Borrowed Stilettos

by

Rebecca J. Clark

This is a work of fiction. Names, characters, places, and incidents either are the product of the author's imagination or are used fictitiously, and any resemblance to actual persons living or dead, business establishments, events, or locales, is entirely coincidental.

Borrowed Stilettos

COPYRIGHT © 2009 by Rebecca J. Clark

All rights reserved. No part of this book may be used or reproduced in any manner whatsoever without written permission of the author or The Wild Rose Press except in the case of brief quotations embodied in critical articles or reviews.
Contact Information: info@thewildrosepress.com

Cover Art by *Nicola Martinez*

The Wild Rose Press
PO Box 708
Adams Basin, NY 14410-0706
Visit us at www.thewildrosepress.com

Publishing History
First Champagne Rose Edition, 2010
Print *ISBN:* 1-60154-764-1

Published in the United States of America

Dedication

To Dan for always believing,
even when I didn't. I love you.

Praise for *Borrowed Stilettos*

2008 RWA Golden Heart Finalist

CHAPTER 1

Audrey Thompson pushed aside her nerves as she slammed the car door, and strode across the cobblestone driveway toward the Banister family mansion. Her ankles wobbled in the borrowed heels and she stumbled, flailing her arms for balance. Her gaze darted around the Sun Valley estate. She was alone, thank goodness. Unfortunately, the movement had dislodged one of her fake boobs. *Crap*!

She dipped her hand into her low-cut blouse and adjusted, praying no one watched from inside the house. She shimmied her shoulders to make sure the falsies stayed put.

She really needed to be more careful. Her sister's career, not to mention Audrey's own pride, was at stake.

Anxiety pretzeled in her belly, and she pressed her hand against it. What the heck had she gotten herself into? If she couldn't pull off the rickety stilettos, salon hair, and phony cleavage, Zachary Banister would know the rest of her was fake, too.

And he'd realize she wasn't the woman he wanted to marry.

Ava was *so* going to owe her.

A mix of weathered wood, stone and glass, the house loomed over her, waiting to swallow her whole. The many windows reflected the mountain sun like prying eyes that saw right through her charade.

Resisting the urge to shiver, she dragged her heavy suitcases to the massive double doors. She could do this. She forced a deep breath of courage. She *would* do this. Raising her hand to the ugly gargoyle door knocker, she rapped three times before she could change her mind and return to Boise.

"I have confidence in confidence alone," she quoted. She frowned. "Yeah, right. And my name isn't Audrey Thompson."

She caught herself. Her name *wasn't* Audrey—at least not for this weekend. For the next few days she was her twin sister, Ava Divine, flight attendant for the rich and famous, actress, and lingerie model.

Audrey swallowed. As if anyone in their right mind would believe that. *She* was afraid of flying. *She* was a junior high school teacher. *She* wore white cotton underwear.

But not today.

The doors swung open. She'd expected Zach Banister to greet her. Instead she found herself staring at a tall, thin man dressed in a tuxedo, with slicked white hair and cheeks pinched as though he sucked on sour candy.

Oh, God. A butler. "We're not in Kansas anymore, Toto," she mumbled.

"Excuse me, Miss?"

She cleared her throat. "I'm, uh, Ava Divine."

"Of course you are," he said, giving her a discreet once-over with his expressionless gaze. He even had a British accent. "I am Stoudt, the Banister family butler."

Stoudt. She would have smiled, but she was afraid of cracking the makeup the real Ava had applied, with what felt like an air compressor and paint roller, a few hours ago. Her lips twitched, while her insides danced a jitterbug.

"I thought butlers went the way of black and white movies," she said as he reached for her two big suitcases, a ridiculous number for a three-day stay. *Her* things would require a single overnight bag.

"We are a dying breed, I'm afraid," he told her.

Thank God they're not completely extinct, she thought as he hoisted the luggage with an undignified grunt. He glanced at her legs as he straightened. Another first. She didn't make a habit of wearing skirts short enough to be on the verge of illegal. Self-consciously, she tugged the hem of the soft leather mini over her thighs.

She only had to make it through one weekend of playing pretend. Audrey stepped past Stoudt as he motioned her inside. The front doors opened into a two-story foyer, with a massive split staircase rising up in front of her like Poseidon, waiting to crush her with a tidal wave. A river rock fireplace, big enough to walk through, divided the foyer from the living area. Audrey gaped at the wood pillars and beams, hardwoods and tiles. Oh, God. She cringed at the thought of navigating those floors in four-inch heels.

The faint scent of lemon oil wafted on the air. A house this size would have a fulltime housekeeper...or two.

"Follow me, please," said Stoudt. "I will show you to your room."

Audrey's heels clicked shrilly against the tiles, then morphed into a muted tapping as the floor transitioned to wide-planked wood. She kept her weight in her toes, taking baby steps so she wouldn't slip.

She waddled behind Stoudt. "Where's Zach—um, Mr. Banister—um, Zach?" What the heck should she call him? "Zach" sounded too familiar, considering she'd never met the man. "Mr. Banister" sounded more correct, but if she was supposed to be his girlfriend, and soon-to-be fiancée...Yikes!

Stoudt started up the wooden stairs and said, without turning around, "Mr. Banister will meet with you at his convenience."

Swell. Maybe her mission here wouldn't be so hard after all. Spoon-fed, arrogant males like Zach Banister deserved what they had coming to them. Still, she'd promised Ava she would be gentle. "Gentle is my middle name," she mumbled, staring up the long staircase and wondering how on earth she'd get to the top without stumbling. She grabbed the polished log railing for balance and life preservation.

Stoudt paused on the landing. He stared at her from beneath raised white brows, and his thin lips squished into a tight knot. "What was that, Miss?"

"Uh, nothing. I just commented on how many steps there are."

He dismissed her with a curt shake of his head as they continued their trek up the stairs. After traveling to the end of a hallway wider than Audrey's entire house, Stoudt stopped in front of a raised-panel door. He set down one suitcase and turned the doorknob.

"Your room, Miss Divine."

"Room" was an understatement. And, thank God, a thick nature-print rug covered those blasted hardwoods nearly wall to wall. Her spiky heels sank deep into the mat as she stepped into the room.

"Dinner will be served punctually at eight. Mrs. Banister will expect you to be dressed *appropriately* for the occasion." He swept a haughty gaze over her, from the white silk blouse with its plunging neckline, all the way down to her red stilettos.

Audrey wondered if this sort of reaction was normal for Ava.

Cocking her head, she studied him. "Do you ever let loose with a big belly laugh?"

Not even a smirk. "Is there anything else you need, Miss?"

That answered her question. "No, thank you. I'm fine. Um, Stoudt," she said, "What should I do between now and dinner?"

He gave her a look that said he thought she was about as smart as a marshmallow. "You may do, Miss, whatever it is that you do." And he closed the door.

What the heck did that mean?

Checking her watch, she realized she had three hours until dinner. Sitting on the edge of the huge lodge-pole bed, she slid her feet out of the uncomfortable heels. A blissful groan slipped from her mouth as she wriggled her bare toes into the rug. "Ah, heaven."

Her gaze traveled to the rustic stone fireplace across the room. And to the enormous deer head hung above the mantle. "My head might be up there beside yours if I'm not careful."

After the almost three-hour drive from Boise to Sun Valley, the beautiful quilt and fluffy pillows beckoned her from the bed. Did she have time for a nap? Probably, but then she'd need to redo her hair and makeup. No.

She paced the floor in her bare feet. What if she screwed up, and Zach Banister found out who she really was? What if she got all tongue-tied, and couldn't do what she was here to do?

"Oh, stop it," she chided herself. She had pretended to be her sister before. Sure, it had been a good fifteen years since the last time, but how hard was it to impersonate someone who looked almost exactly like her, someone she'd known her entire life?

She reviewed what Ava had told her about Zach. He was thirty-two, the only son of Garrett and Grace Banister, founders of some big investment firm on the East Coast. The family also owned an executive aircraft company, which Zach managed. Ava was a flight attendant on the chartered jet trips he often piloted.

He was known to mix with the likes of celebrities and supermodels. *Gag.* He'd pretty much been raised by nannies and governesses. *Yuck.* He had one older sister, owned an apartment in Manhattan, and a condo on Maui. And, according to her sister, his last relationship had resulted in a nasty breakup.

A nasty breakup. Great. He was about to have another. Audrey's gut clenched. Glancing at the ornate clock beneath the deer head, she decided to go downstairs. They certainly didn't expect her to remain in her room until dinner, did they?

She glared at the stilettos she'd discarded by the door. Bare feet were fine for Audrey, but Ava lived and breathed by her shoe fetish. She wrestled back her nerves, and mashed her feet back into the horrible heels. "Be Ava, be Ava, be Ava."

She hobbled down the hall and paused at the top of the stairs, hearing voices below.

Two women and a man stood in the foyer, talking. The famous Banisters. Their voices were too low to make out the words, but the women, the older one in particular, looked upset. From the rigid way his arms crossed over his broad chest, the man didn't seem too pleased either.

Audrey swallowed. That must be Zach.

A funny little shiver skittered across her skin. Ava had described him as male perfection. Audrey had seen his pictures, but the photos and Ava's description didn't do him justice. His body would make the Greek gods bow down in reverence to wide shoulders that spoke of good genetics and hard workouts, a chest that begged to be pressed against, and a lower body that looked way too yummy in blue jeans. Why on earth did her sister want to break up with *that*?

Well. It was now or never. Adrenaline blasted through her veins, heating her skin. Taking a deep breath of courage, she navigated the first step downward while holding the banister for support. Her ankle wobbled on the four-inch heel. She took another step. This time, she swayed precariously. Her head swam with visions of being splayed out like road kill on the Banister slate.

The threesome below turned her way.

"Ava," Zach greeted with a smile in his voice. Its

deep tone echoed the answering quiver in her belly. She imagined what *her* name would sound like rolling off his tongue. She froze on the second step from the top, afraid to move. Who in their right mind would ever install hardwood stairs? Nerves rattled around her gut like coins in an empty soda can.

"Darling, we were just talking about you," he said, moving toward the bottom of the staircase.

Darling? Oh, crap. How was she supposed to break up with a man who called her 'darling' in such a sexy way?

"Come down here, and I'll introduce you."

Judging from the hostile postures of the women, Audrey decided she'd rather have a root canal. She hoped they couldn't see up her skirt from their lower vantage point. She said a silent prayer of thanks she hadn't taken her sister's advice and was, in fact, wearing panties. Could she call a thong "panties"?

Zach's dark brows pulled together over his puzzled stare. He jogged up to her, stopping a couple of steps below. "What's going on?" he whispered.

She met his gaze. Oh, God. He had the most beautiful blue eyes she'd ever seen. "N-Nothing," she stammered, and forced herself to breathe. A heady combination of citrus and musk assailed her. He smelled so good she wanted to bury her face against his shoulder and inhale.

She couldn't tell him the truth. That she'd never worn shoes this stacked in her life. That she was a sneakers girl. She dug her long fingernails into the fleshy part of her palm to remind herself to get a grip on reality. He wasn't *her* boyfriend.

Those gorgeous eyes narrowed. Deep, piercing blue, and fringed with black lashes and laugh lines. Up close, he was even better looking than in the tabloids, movie-star handsome with just a hint of stubble on his strong chin. His black hair gleamed blue in the sunlight streaming through the large windows. She wondered how it would feel in her hands. She rubbed her suddenly damp palms against her thighs.

A rumble of something purely primal roiled deep in her belly. From this proximity, she could see his hair was just starting to gray at the temples, adding to his good looks. When she got her first gray hair, she was certain it wouldn't add to her looks.

Her sister was insane.

Something flickered in his eyes as he stared at her. *Oh, God. He knows I'm not Ava.* She raised an eyebrow and met his gaze squarely, hoping she looked confident.

A grin tugged at his lips and he reached for her hand, entwining their fingers. Absorbed in the physical contact and in looking at his mouth, she forgot to move her feet, and lost her balance. Her arms flailed, and she found herself chest to chest with Zachary Banister.

"Whoa there, tiger," he said. He chuckled, his breath warm against her ear.

For the first time today, she was glad for the falsies, otherwise the only thing between her breasts and him would be the lacy excuse of a bra and the silky fabric of her blouse. Her nipples pebbled. Clearly, she'd been without a man too long.

His hand slid down her back, all the way down to her backside. He squeezed, and Audrey's pulse cartwheeled through her veins.

"Kiss me," he murmured, lowering his face.

Of all the rude, chauvinistic—Wait. Holy crap! He was touching her butt! The way his hands burned through her clothes, she might as well be naked. Warmth spread outward from his hand like slow-moving lava, until every square inch of her skin tingled.

At the last minute, she turned her head. "M-My lipstick," she muttered, conscious of his family watching. "I, uh, just put it on."

His lips thinned, and a spark of annoyance

flickered through his deep blue eyes. "Forget the lipstick, Ava. Remember what we talked about."

Ava. Under usual circumstances, Audrey would never be mistaken for her prettier and sexier sister. And what did he mean, what they had they talked about? She scanned her memory for everything Ava had told her.

"Yes, absolutely I remember," she lied, smiling up at him. Audrey glanced away, worried if he looked too closely he'd see she was an imposter. Worried if *she* looked too closely, she might wrap her legs around his waist and beg him to take her right now, right here. Instead, she looked straight ahead at his chest. His white button-down shirt was open just enough at the collar to reveal a sprinkling of coarse, black hair. Her palms itched as she imagined running her hands over his bare skin, the coarse hairs tickling her.

Okay, she'd look at the windows behind him, or anywhere that didn't elicit heat to flush her face and pool in the pit of her stomach. And lower.

He propped one foot on the stair beside her and pressed his hand into the small of her back, welding their hips. This time, she didn't pull away. She couldn't really, with his hands on her. What would he do if she rocked her pelvis against his? How would his body react? Hmm. Tempting.

What on earth was wrong with her?

Zach's warm breath mingled with hers as he leaned in to kiss her. Their lips touched, and she swayed on her Manolo-something shoes. He angled his head and teased the closed seam of her lips with his tongue. Her head hummed and excitement rippled across her skin. She gripped his arms, ready to kiss him back, when he pulled away.

His eyes narrowed, creating a furrow between his brows. *He knows something's different!*

He cocked his head. "Hmm," he said, then reached for her hand and guided her down the stairs, like the embrace had never happened.

How could he be so calm, when her entire being quivered like children on the first day of school? Of course, he'd kissed her sister before, so to him this was no big deal. But Audrey had never kissed him. To her, this was momentous.

When they reached the foyer, he dipped his head and whispered in her ear, "You look perfect, by the way."

She couldn't help smiling, despite her anxiety. When was the last time anyone had thought she looked perfect?

He cleared his throat as they approached the women. "Mother, Theresa—"

Mother Theresa? Was impersonating one's sister a sin?

Wrapping his arm around her shoulders and pulling her close to his side, he said, "This is the love of my life, Ava Divine. Ava darling, this is my mother, Grace Banister, and my sister, Theresa."

Ava darling? Love of his life? Oh, God. What had Ava gotten her into? And how could her sister not want to be the love of this man's life?

Mrs. Banister's sleek silver bob framed smooth skin and high cheekbones, the results of great genetics or a skilled plastic surgeon, or both. Her face reminded Audrey of a porcelain doll—flawless, with a half-smile and expressionless eyes.

Audrey put on what she hoped was a genuine smile and held out her hand, complete with a new set of fake fingernails painted hooker red.

Zach's mother looked her up and down, then grasped the ends of her fingers, as if to avoid touching her any more than necessary. Before Audrey could stop herself, she readjusted her grip and gave the matron of the mansion a firm handshake.

With a disapproving glare that actually caused frown lines on her forehead, Mrs. Banister pulled from Audrey's grasp. "Welcome to our home, Miss Divine," she said in a perfectly modulated voice.

"Thank you, and please call me Au—Ava."

Theresa didn't shake Audrey's hand, but crossed her arms over her cream-colored silk blouse, and stared at Audrey from under lifted brows. She shared her mother's regal looks, but with dark hair.

Like her mother, Theresa had that slender and shapeless build akin to the Paris Hiltons of the world, as if they truly believed you could never be too rich or too thin. Audrey shifted from one foot to the other, suddenly self-conscious of her curvier figure.

Zach squeezed her shoulder. She figured it was a silent apology for his family's less than stellar welcome, until she peeked up at him. A faint smile curved the corners of his beautiful mouth, and his eyes twinkled as he peered down at her.

Her legs shook, a combination of nerves and the stilettos. Her sister clearly didn't have her head screwed on straight. The more money a man had, the more Ava usually liked him. If he was good-looking to boot, as Zach so obviously was, that was even better.

But he had apparently broken Ava's cardinal rule—he'd fallen in love with her.

So here Audrey was to do Ava's dirty work, with the hunk-of-the-month standing close enough for her to breathe in his sexy aftershave.

When Zach slipped his hand around her waist and his fingers grazed the side of her breast, Audrey gasped. Time for what her drama students called an 'exit, stage right.'

She backed out of his embrace, teetering on the stilettos. "I, ah, need to go fix my lipstick." She caught Zach's eye for the briefest of moments, then toddled across the foyer to the bottom of the staircase. Her gaze trekked up the steps, then back down to her stupid shoes.

"Oh, what the heck," she muttered, reaching down to slip off the high heels. For one crazy moment, she was tempted to turn around and take a bow. Instead, she sprinted up the stairs.

CHAPTER 2

Zach watched Ava scurry up the curving staircase. His body tightened in response to the sight of her long, toned legs under that sinfully short skirt. He'd never really appreciated what great legs she had. At least she'd had the good sense to take off those ridiculous, but damned sexy, high heels before heading upstairs. Maybe that was what bothered him. Ava rarely showed good sense. Or maybe it was because, for a moment when they'd kissed, he'd been attracted to her and wanted more.

Something wasn't right. He realized his family was about as welcoming as a basket of spitting cobras, but he'd explained the situation to her on the phone last week. She'd seemed fine with meeting them then. Not so much now.

"Do you really expect us to buy that?"

Zach spun and found his mom and sister staring at him, arms crossed. "What do you mean?"

"She means," Grace said, "that Miss Divine doesn't quite fit the mold of your dream girl."

"You have no clue what my idea of a dream girl is," he told them. Neither did he.

"Well, it's clearly not her," Theresa said, nodding toward the upper hallway where Ava had disappeared. "The chemistry between you is about as genuine as her bust line." Theresa's well-bred brows rose.

Damn. Maybe he should have chosen a woman he had more passion for than Ava. But she was otherwise perfect. He and Ava would have to step it up a notch if he wanted this charade to work.

****

"Ava, what the heck have you gotten me into?" Audrey hissed into her cell phone. She stood at the window in her room, squinting into the bright May sunshine.

A faint grating sound buzzed through the receiver, and she realized her sister was filing her nails. "I told you exactly what you were getting into, and you agreed." Ava's sultry voice would make a grocery list sound sexy.

"You begged me to help you."

"You could have said no."

When had Audrey ever said no to her twin? Not in this lifetime. "Yeah, whatever. But you're going to owe me big-time for this." Her back bedroom overlooked a huge, kidney-shaped pool. A stamped-concrete path encircled the sparkling water, and opened into an expansive patio dotted with chaise lounges and umbrellas. It looked more like a posh resort than a private backyard.

She heard her sister blow onto her fingernails. "He's cute, isn't he?" Ava asked.

Audrey's pulse blipped. "Cute doesn't begin to describe him. He's...perfect." She ran a finger along the polished wooden sill, then studied the faint smudge left behind by her skin.

Ava sighed. "Yeah. He's a hottie. Too bad he had to go and get all serious on me. Have you taken care of business yet?"

"I've been here less than an hour, Ava."

"You've always prided yourself on being so efficient, sis. Am I finally beginning to rub off on you? God can only hope..."

Audrey couldn't help chuckling. "You've not only rubbed off on me, I've *become* you. You'd be proud of me so far. I've done well, except for tripping on the stairs."

"Aud-*reeey*. You need to be more careful. You're going to give yourself away."

Audrey chewed on her lower lip. "Yeah, well, you

were born wearing stilettos." She turned away from the window, and plopped into an over-stuffed chair. She stretched out her legs and admired the pedicure Ava had insisted she get. She wriggled her red-tipped toes, and the gloss caught the sunlight through the windows.

"So, when will you do it?" Ava asked.

"Yo. Is your head screwed on straight? Why on earth do you want to break up with him?"

"He would be perfect, except for the teensy tiny fact that he said the 'F' word to me."

"What?"

"Yeah, you know. 'Fiancée'?"

Audrey hinged forward in the chair. "Oh. My. God. A rich, handsome man is in love with you. Call 911."

"Who said anything about love?"

Audrey dreamt of falling madly in love some day, with a man who would adore her in and out of the bedroom. Zach's face appeared in her mind's mirror. She mentally fogged the glass. "He must be in love with you if he wants to marry you." Silence echoed in her ear. "Ava? You still there?"

"Oh, yeah," came the distracted reply. "Off! Down! Your dog keeps jumping on my lap."

"He likes you."

"The feeling's *not* mutual. His hairs are sticking to my clothes. It's really disgusting. So, when will you do it?" Ava returned to the original conversation as if she'd never disrupted it.

"I'm pacing myself. I still can't believe you talked me into breaking up with Zachary Banister for you. Do you know how many women in this country would love to be in your shoes?"

"No, no, no. You know how horrible I am at confrontation. If I screw it up, I'll lose my job."

Audrey cringed at the thought. Her sister had the perfect career for her lifestyle—she regularly flew to exotic locales, and got to hobnob with rich and famous people. It would be a shame if Ava lost that.

"Remember when I tried to break up with Robbie Calendar?" Ava asked. "I did so bad, he started crying."

"Yeah, well, guys don't really appreciate being told they bore the crap out of you."

"See, that's why I need *you*. You're way nicer than me. When you pretended to be me and broke up with Robbie, you did such a good job that he and I stayed friends."

"And when he found out I'd impersonated you, he told his parents, who told our parents, and I was grounded for two months." Audrey hoped *this* attempt didn't have similar negative results. For her. Somehow, Ava always came out okay.

"Yeah." Ava sounded wistful. "I always did feel kind of bad about that."

Right, Audrey thought.

"What's the big deal?" Ava asked. "How many times have you told me how boring your life is, and how nothing exciting ever happens to you?"

"This isn't quite what I had in mind."

"You're always telling me to make the best of things. Maybe you should take your own advice. Have fun while you're there. Live it up. Without blowing your cover, of course."

"Breaking up with a man I don't know is hardly my idea of a good time."

"Speaking of *not* blowing your cover, have you memorized my list?"

Audrey sighed. "You wrote it down for me."

"Let me hear it."

"I don't want to—" She knew better than to argue with her stubborn twin. "Fine. I'll get it."

She rose from the comfortable chair, then strode to the suitcase she hadn't bothered unpacking. She didn't plan on being in Sun Valley long enough to justify the headache.

Reaching under a stack of clothes, she retrieved a folded piece of paper with the heading, *Ava's Absolutes*. "Okay. Number one. Never be seen without makeup or hair done. Any time. Anywhere. Number two. Stilettos are a girl's best friend. No matter the occasion."

She glowered at the nasty shoes lying next to the door. "Uh, not *this* girl's best friend. How the heck can you stand wearing such high heels?"

"How can you stand not to? Go on."

Audrey blew an exasperated breath, and sat on the edge of the bed. "Never let him see you in sweats. A chipped nail on the fingers or toes should be a crime. Thong or commando. Enough said." That last absolute prompted her to squirm on the mattress.

"Good," Ava said. "If you can remember the list, you'll be fine."

Audrey doubted it. There was nothing "fine" about breaking up with a man while wearing underpanties that felt like dental floss.

****

Zach rapped his knuckles against Ava's door. "It's open," she called from inside.

He opened the door, but stayed in the doorway.

"Oh. Hi," she said when she saw him.

"I came up here to check on you. You ran away so quickly." He looked her up and down, his gaze lingering on her bare legs and feet. Damn if his heart rate didn't speed up a notch at the sight.

"I'm fine," she said, her voice a bit breathless.

He smiled. "I can see that." More than fine.

"This is a beautiful house, Mr.—ah—Zach. Does your family live here year-round?"

"We spend much of the ski season here, of course, and we're always in town for Saturday's Memorial Weekend golf tournament. Do you golf, Ava?"

"No, actually." Her long lashes swept across her

downcast eyes. "I've never tried it."

Her answer didn't surprise him. Ava Divine probably didn't do anything that could break a nail. "You can come along and watch, or you can hang out here. May I come in?" At her nod, he stepped inside the room. "Have you had a chance to look around?" His gaze lingered on the bed. He'd never been in Ava's bedroom before. He'd never wanted to be. So why had his breathing suddenly shallowed?

She shook her head. "Jeeves brought me straight to my room when I arrived. We didn't pass Go, nor did we collect $200."

With anyone else, Zach might have chuckled. But not with her. Ava Divine rarely made jokes. He cocked his head and studied her. Somehow, in the weeks since he'd last seen her, she'd morphed into a kinder, gentler, funnier Ava. A hell of a lot sexier, too.

Exactly what he didn't want, or need, this weekend. He'd chosen Ava primarily because she wasn't his type. Damn.

Maybe his family's behavior affected her more than he'd expected. "I know I warned you about my family, but I'll apologize for them anyway. You get my mother and Theresa together, and they're worse than Donald Trump in his boardroom."

She blinked, and her black lashes fanned her cheekbones. He couldn't know for sure, but they were probably as artificial as several other things about her. He liked that in a woman...at least in this case.

"Speaking of your family, Stoudt mentioned that your mom expects me to dress appropriately for dinner. What would you suggest?"

When had he ever known her to ask his or anyone else's opinion on how to dress? Ava Divine dressed however she damn well pleased. "What you're wearing now will be just fine." His gaze traveled from her low-cut blouse to the leather skirt so snug it cupped her behind. His hands itched to do the same.

"Really? I got the impression from your butler that this wasn't okay."

His head buzzed with confusion. He moved close and gripped her arms. "What's gotten into you?" A highlighted lock of hair fell across her brow. He peered into her eyes. He'd never noticed they were the exact color of the mountain stream that ran alongside his cabin. He shook the thought from his mind. "You're acting really...different."

"Um, I guess I'm just a little nervous about this weekend."

"Since when do you get nervous?"

"Like you said, your family is pretty intimidating. I don't want to make a fool of myself."

Still clutching her arms, he felt unexpected muscle tone. Had she been working out, or had it really been that long since he'd held her? "Ava. Look at me."

She did, and her beautiful eyes sucked him in like the vortex of a tornado. He released her and shoved his hands into his pockets, then pulled them out again. He crossed his arms over his chest. What the hell was wrong with him? He stepped back. "Just be yourself, and you'll be fine."

"Be myself? That's easier said than done," she murmured, turning away.

While part of him panicked over this unwelcome change in her personality and his unexpected attraction to her, another part of him, the testosterone-driven part of him, admired her bare legs and feet. His hands yearned to glide up those toned thighs and under that short skirt.

Turned on by Ava Divine. Another first.

He forced his gaze from her figure, and glanced around the room. A photo album lay open on the rumpled bedspread. He crossed the floor and reached for it. "What's this?"

"Oh, no!" she shrieked. "Don't look at that." She yanked it out of his hands and pressed the book against her chest, shielding it from his eyes.

But he'd already seen the pictures inside, and he heaved a huge sigh of relief. "You have an entire album filled with pictures of yourself?" This was just what he would expect from the Ava Divine he knew.

Her cheeks turned red, then a familiar flash of fire sparked in her eyes. "This photo album is my business. Not yours."

He grinned and headed for the door. "You should relax before dinner. Trust me—you'll need all your wits about you." *And then some.* Pausing within the doorframe, he said, "Oh, by the way. That trip on the stairs was priceless. But next time, warn me ahead of time. I almost didn't catch you."

She stared at him, unblinking. "Oh. Right."

"One more thing." He glanced at her luscious mouth, and her pink tongue slipped out to moisten her lips. His groin flexed, and he shifted his stance. "We really need to work on our kissing."

****

Stoudt stood, guard-like, at the bottom of the stairs as Audrey descended for dinner. His disapproving gaze told her she'd failed on the "dress appropriately" requirement.

"Oh, come on, Stoudt. Cut me some slack," she said.

He gave an undignified little snort under his breath, but she thought the corner of his mouth tugged upward.

She'd chosen the most benign outfit of the bunch—black leather pants, and an off-the-shoulder gypsy blouse in flaming red. She had to admit, as much as she disliked Ava's taste in clothing, she admired its quality. The way the fine material brushed against her skin as she moved, the way the butter-soft leather molded to her bottom and thighs. It was all quite...sensual. No wonder *she* was a good girl—most of *her* clothing was cotton.

As Stoudt led her to the dining room, she felt like Daniel approaching the lion's den. She took comfort in remembering that Daniel came out the victor in the end. She didn't take comfort knowing he'd had to slay a lot of lions first.

Her stomach churned as she eyed the Banister family gathered around a massive wooden table. A distinguished-looking older man sat at one end with a scowl on his tanned face. Zach's dad, if the close resemblance was any indication. His mother sat at the other end looking as cool, elegant and refined as Audrey remembered. Theresa and an unfamiliar man, presumably her husband, sat on one side of the table. Zach sat alone across from them, an empty chair beside him. Her chair. *Gulp.* Her insides fluttered like the wings of a hummingbird.

His eyes met hers, and for a moment, Audrey stood on a movie screen where everything receded out of focus except for one thing. That one thing smiled. She hoped she managed to return the gesture.

The family stood as Stoudt announced her presence. Each of them looked like they'd stepped out of *Town and Country* magazine, and each seemed to have a disdain in their eyes just for her. Except for Zach, who pushed back his chair and circled the table.

"Darling!" he said, sliding his arm around her waist. His hands found bare skin, and she sucked in her breath at the unexpected contact. She forced a neutral expression onto her face, even though her insides danced with nerves. He kissed her cheek. "Everyone, I want you to meet Ava Divine. Ava, meet the rest of my family." He went around the room with introductions. She didn't pay much attention, too focused on where he touched her.

All in all, the group was about as warm and cuddly as a group autopsy. Thank God Ava didn't want to marry into this family, because then, they'd be *her* family. Yikes!

Finally, Zach led her to the chair beside his. As Audrey sat, Stoudt materialized behind her and offered her a choice of wines.

"You have anything that comes in a screw top?" she muttered.

Laughter sparkled in the butler's eyes a moment before he returned to his customary deadpan. "No, Miss. Our wine cellar obviously needs restocking. I hope these will be an adequate substitute?"

None of the wine labels looked familiar. "They're fine. How about the white, please?"

At the far end of the table, Mrs. Banister cleared her throat. "Your last name is quite unusual, Ava. Tell me, is it your given name?"

Audrey took a long drink. The wine warmed her throat and belly. It even tasted expensive, smooth and rich, unlike the bitter bottles she had at home. "No, actually. I was born Ava Thompson. Divine is my, ah, stage name."

Mrs. Banister's perfectly arched eyebrows rose. "Are you an actress?" She practically spat the term.

Audrey scraped her brain to come up with an appropriate Ava response. "I've, ah, done some acting, but I started using that name when I began my modeling career. Ava Divine sounded more glamorous and exciting than Ava Thompson."

"Yes," Mrs. Banister drawled. "I'm sure it did."

Theresa sat across from Audrey. "We know absolutely nothing about you, Ava." She pressed her fingers to her throat and gave a little laugh, glancing around the table. "You'd think Zach would have told us *everything*, but he hasn't said a word. It's almost like you didn't exist before today." She directed a pointed look at Zach, while the insult sank into Audrey's head.

Zach tensed beside her. How could he stand having such a horrible family? She waited for his response, but none came.

Grace said, "Yes, do tell us about yourself, Ava."

Forcing a pleasant expression, Audrey asked, "What do you want to know?"

"Your parents. What do they do?"

"My parents died when I was in college." And they were probably turning over in their graves right now at the mess their daughter was in.

"You're an orphan." Zach's mother gave her what she probably thought was a sympathetic smile.

Audrey struggled to control her temper and lost. "Yes, I'm an orphan. My only family now are Daddy Warbucks and my dog, Sandy."

Brows went up around the table. She refused to look Zach's way until he squeezed her knee. She'd expected him to be angry, but he looked like he was biting back a grin.

"Little Orphan Ava?" he asked. His grin escaped.

Her lips curled into a return smile. "Something like that," she said, catching and holding his gaze. Her naughty side wished he'd move his hand a bit further north. The area between her legs throbbed at the thought.

And if he did? She'd either pass out in shock, or her gasp of pleasure would embarrass her in front of his family. Every centimeter of her skin burned beneath his touch.

Polite laughter twittered around the table as if she'd meant the comment to be funny.

Zach removed his hand from her leg, and she immediately felt its loss. She supposed she wanted to continue clinging to the one person here who didn't seem to hate her guts.

Dinner passed slower than slugs on ice. Early on, Audrey made the decision to keep her mouth shut unless spoken to, and then keep her answers short and to the point. After that first round of questions, no one made an effort to speak to her.

Zach's father grilled him on the aviation business. He didn't seem to warm to the topic, and alternated between looks of boredom and anger. Maybe his family annoyed him, too.

How sad, she thought, to have a family you didn't enjoy. She wished she had *more* family to spend time with. It was just her and Ava, whom she didn't see nearly as often as she would have liked.

As dessert arrived, Zach dinged his fork against the side of his wine glass and stood. "Could I have everyone's attention, please?"

All talk ceased, and everyone stared at Zach. And Audrey.

Flustered, with the warmth of embarrassment and fine wine buzzing her cheeks, Audrey peered at him.

He grinned a crooked grin that would have left 99.9% of the female population a worthless puddle of mush on the floor—her included. He brandished a small velvet box from his pocket, and dropped to one knee beside her chair.

Oh. My. God.

He flipped open the box to reveal a breathtaking ring, a massive diamond surrounded by gazillions of smaller ones. They glittered beneath the lights of the chandelier. He took it out and reached for her hand. Slipping the heavy ring onto her finger, he said, "Ava, my love. Would you do me the honor of becoming my wife, and making me the happiest man in the world?"

The room grew pin-drop silent. Audrey heard only the drumming of her heart and the blood pulsing through her veins.

Her sister hadn't warned her about *this*!

Zach stared at her, his expression slightly pleading. Odd. Could he see in her eyes that she planned to reject him? How would he react when she said 'no'? Would he be gracious, and able to hide his disappointment and shock? Or would his heart break right in front of her?

Audrey's heart squeezed, and compassionate tears stung the backs of her eyelids.

She sensed everyone's attention on her. Just one little word and she'd be out of here, away from this nasty family and the uncomfortable shoes. She could be back on the road to Boise within the hour.

Her heart gave an unexpected leap in her chest.

Just one little word.

Unfortunately, she chose the wrong one. "Yes."

CHAPTER 3

"You did *what?*" Ava shrieked into the phone.

Audrey held the receiver away from her ear, but could still hear her sister's rant. "I didn't mean to say yes, Ava. It just...popped out."

"How can agreeing to marry someone just 'pop' out?"

"I couldn't help it. I mean, no one has ever asked me to marry him before, and I guess I just...got caught up in the moment." The explanation sounded lame even to her ears. How could she explain what she didn't understand herself?

"Besides," she continued, "he was down on bent knee, for goodness' sake. His whole family was watching. I didn't want to embarrass him by saying no." She held up her hand to admire the ring he'd slipped onto her finger at dinner. She turned it this way and that, watching the diamonds catch the light. It was beautiful, but she'd have preferred something less ostentatious. Less...Ava-like.

"You could have said, 'Let's talk about this in private.' You could have said anything but 'Yes.' Gawd, Audrey, this is my life we're talking about here. I'm not marrying him!"

"Calm down, will you? No one is saying you have to marry him...but if you wanted the breakup done right, well, you know the old saying."

"Aud-*reeeey*! I don't want a fiancé."

Neither did Audrey. Breaking up with a fiancé was a little different than breaking up with a boyfriend. A wave of nausea roiled through her stomach. *A lot* different. "Okay, okay," she said. "I'll take care of it."

But for the life of her, she had no idea how.

After hanging up, she sat on the edge of the king-size bed, curling and uncurling her fingers into the quilt. She'd come to Sun Valley with a purpose: to break up with Zachary Banister. A relatively simple, if uncomfortable, task. She performed more difficult duties every day in her job. Breaking up with a man she didn't even know should have been far easier than spending six hours a day, five days a week with pre-teens in hormonal hell.

"Should have" being the key words.

"Crap," she muttered, standing and pacing to the window. She moved aside the heavy curtains and peered outside. Darkness had settled over the valley. Lights from the resort town twinkled in the distance, and Audrey wished she was anywhere but here.

She drummed her fake fingernails on the windowsill. All she'd had to do was say no to Ava about this weekend. All she'd had to do was say no to Zach about his proposal. Crap!

Think. Think! How could she get out of this? She pressed her forehead against the cool pane, and her breath fogged the glass. There was no graceful way to tell your fiancé that you wanted out of the relationship. This should be easy; he wasn't really *her* fiancé. Still, she didn't want to hurt him unnecessarily.

She made a dismissive sound under her breath. From everything Ava had told her about him, and from what she'd read in the tabloids, he wouldn't have the slightest qualm about breaking up with her if the roles were reversed. He'd probably broken up with scores of women, and not given it a second thought.

Yes! She straightened and grinned. She simply had to convince him to break up with *her*.

But how? She dropped into the overstuffed chair beside the windows, and rested her chin in her hands. The Banister family clearly wasn't crazy about Ava Divine. Every man, no matter his age, cared about his family's opinion, didn't they? Elegant, classy and reserved people like the Banisters wanted elegant, classy and reserved partners for their children. Pretty much the opposite of Ava.

Audrey stretched out her arms, interlaced palms outward, readying for battle. This plan would take every ounce of her drama-teaching experience. She'd deserve an Oscar by the end of the weekend, if everything went as she hoped.

"Look out, Banister family. You ain't seen *nothin'* yet."

She waited until everyone had gone to bed. She checked her reflection in the mirror one last time, and grinned in spite of her nervousness. Perfect. If she played her cards right, she'd be heading back to Boise come morning light.

Asking her inner Oz for courage, she opened the door and stepped into the hall.

"Let the show begin," she muttered. "By the time I'm done with you, Zach, you'll be *begging* me for your ring back."

****

Zach turned off the water and listened, his mouth full of mouthwash.

"Zachary! Oh, Zaaachareee!" Ava, yelling his name at the top of her lungs. At several decibels above considerate, she began pounding on doors.

Zach spat the mouthwash into the sink, then rushed into the hall, still holding his towel, chest bare, and jeans unbuttoned. His mouth dropped open.

Ava stood at the opposite end of the hall, wearing nothing but high-heeled mules and a very short red robe, the silky kind with feathery trim. He wondered what, if anything, she wore beneath it. Her long, wavy hair cascaded loose over her shoulders in a sexy, appealing mess. She gripped a bottle of champagne.

"Zachary, baby. Where are you? This house is just so big, I can't find your room." She lifted the bottle to her lips, and took a long swig.

Just as Zach opened his mouth to call her, his father burst from his room across the hall. "For chrissake, Miss Divine. It's after midnight. You can see Zachary in the morning."

She turned at the sound of his father's raging voice, but her gaze went to Zach. "Darling, there you are. I've been looking everywhere for you."

She pushed past the senior Banister, and flung herself into Zach's arms. Soft red lips pressed against his mouth, and her leg hooked around his hip as her momentum slammed them against the wall.

Zach's body hardened immediately at the feel of her long, lithe body wrapped around him. She tasted of champagne and mint, as if she'd just brushed her teeth. He wanted nothing more than to yank her into his room and finish what she'd started.

Garrett cleared his throat, bringing Zach back to reality. His family had poked their heads out of their bedrooms to watch with a mixture of curiosity and annoyance. He couldn't meet Theresa's gaze; he knew she'd be giving him her perfected "big sister glare."

He bit back a grin. Life couldn't get much better than this.

"Ava, *darling*," he murmured against her mouth. "We've got an audience."

She pulled away, her green eyes wide, and slapped a hand over her luscious lips. "Oops. Silly me," she said. "Sorry, folks. I was just looking for my man. You can go back to bed now." To Zach, she said, "Come on, stud," and tugged him into his room, kicking the door shut behind them with her heel.

Alone with him in his room, Audrey froze, unsure what to do next. She turned, expecting to see outrage in his eyes. Instead, she found him grinning like a kid on Christmas morning.

"Oh, my God, Ava," he said with a laugh. "You should have seen the looks on everyone's faces as you traipsed down the hallway in that getup."

Audrey frowned. What?

His laughter quieted, and he placed his hands on his hips, giving her the once-over. "I guarantee everyone was wondering just what you have on under that robe." His gaze swept over her body, making her want to tighten the sash. If she was bolder, she'd treat him to a similar perusal, let her eyes linger on that broad, bare chest and the way the dark, curly hair thinned into a path that led right to his unbuttoned jeans....

She pulled her gaze from dangerous territory. "Uh, do you want me to leave?"

"Since you're here, and you brought champagne, we might as well have a glass." He took the bottle.

"You're not mad at me?"

"God, no. I've never been happier."

"O-kay."

He crossed to the bar and pulled out two champagne flutes. He had a personal bar in his bedroom? Well, of course he did. Rich people could have whatever they wanted.

He motioned to a pair of French doors leading to a deck. "Let's take this outside, shall we? We can celebrate."

Damn. Damn, and double damn. Reluctantly, she followed him outside. A welcoming mountain breeze wrapped itself around her arms and bare legs.

Now she was stuck in Zach's bedroom, wearing nothing but lingerie and high heels. And the champagne was flowing. You put a man, a woman, champagne, and skimpy lingerie together, and what did you get?

Deep doo-doo. She needed more of that

champagne.

Zach handed her a glass of bubbly liquid, his fingers grazing hers. She met his penetrating gaze, and goosebumps rose on her skin. She wished she could read his mind. Did he think she was crazy, as she'd hoped? His gaze dropped to her mouth, and she stopped breathing. Did he want to kiss her? Should she let him if he tried?

No. Her mission to break up with him did not include throwing herself at him, no matter what her body desired.

"You're shivering," he said softly. "Want to go back inside?"

She shook her head and moved to the railing, draining half her glass of champagne, hoping to build her courage. Her head started to get that warm and fuzzy feeling it got when she'd had a bit much to drink. When Zach's arm slid across her shoulders, she jumped.

"Sorry. You looked cold." He pulled her tighter to his side, his body heat radiating into hers and warming her more than he'd probably intended.

He rubbed his hand up and down her arm, and Audrey swore his touch generated sparks on her skin. She shouldn't enjoy standing so close like this. She shouldn't enjoy the feel of his hard, half-naked body next to her near-nakedness. She should be embarrassed and mortified.

Instead, her body tingled with awareness and vitality, as if she'd just woken up from a fabulous dream.

She glanced sideways at his unbuttoned jeans, and wondered if he wore tighty-whiteys or boxers. Or maybe he preferred going commando. Whatever his preference, the bulge beneath his fly told her he was well-endowed. Her toes curled in the high-heeled mules. She wanted to beg him to *please* fasten that damn, distracting button.

He pulled away and held out his glass. "To us,"

he said, grinning in the dim light.

She found herself holding out her drink in a toast. Her hands shook as she sipped the expensive liquid. The sweet bubbles burst inside her mouth, and some of it dribbled down her chin.

Zach reached out and swiped it away with his thumb. "I have the insane urge to kiss you right now," he said, his voice deep and husky.

She blinked. "Maybe you're insane." Her whisper actually sounded throaty and sexy like the real Ava's.

He chuckled, the sound dancing over her nerves like satin sheets against bare skin. "Maybe." When he leaned toward her, she knew she should run, but only Charlie's Angels could successfully run in high heels.

He grasped her jaw and kissed the corner of her mouth, his tongue flicking away the remainder of the champagne. He pulled back enough to peer into her eyes. "You shouldn't have kissed me like that in the hallway," he murmured.

"I-I shouldn't have?" Audrey replied.

He shook his head, still holding her gaze. "Not unless you wanted me to kiss you again. Like this." He dipped his head and captured her mouth, his tongue skimming along the seam of her lips until she opened to him.

His hand slid around her neck and pulled her closer. Her breasts crushed against his bare chest as he pinned her to the railing. A delicious throb pulsed between her legs, and she knew she should stop this before she got into more trouble. But never had she wanted a moment as much as right now. Excitement and anticipation hummed through her veins.

"God, Ava," he muttered as he moved from her mouth to her neck. He pushed aside the collar of the flimsy robe to nibble the area where her neck and shoulder met. A tingle shot from there all the way down to her toes. "This is insane."

"I warned you," she said, her neck arching back as he dipped his tongue into the hollow of her throat.

She, Audrey Thompson, was kissing Zachary Banister. No, not just kissing, but making out with him with the same amount of abandon and passion as the teenagers she caught necking by their lockers at school. And from the hard ridge pressing against her hip, he got off on it as much as she.

"There's something you haven't told me." His voice vibrated against her neck. "Something I really need to know."

She stiffened and pulled away. "What?" She couldn't meet his eyes.

"What are you wearing under that robe?"

Her heart fluttered. "That's for me to know..." What was she saying?

"Is that an invitation?"

"You're the famous playboy. You figure it out."

His throaty chuckle skimmed over her nerve endings as he backed up a step. The cool breeze that swept across her body quenched her internal fire about as well as dropping an ice cube into a pot of boiling water. He reached for her champagne flute, then set both glasses on a small table beside a chaise lounge. He grasped the sash holding her robe together, rubbing the silky material between his fingers, all the while staring into her eyes.

He tugged, and the filmy fabric parted, revealing her nearly-naked body. She returned his smile despite the good-girl warning bells in her head, too hot to feel anything other than his searing attention.

"Ah," he said. "Black lace."

Her body throbbed in all her intimate places, screaming for his touch even though she knew it was wrong. She should be embarrassed. She barely knew him. Yet her body and mind ached for his next touch.

She didn't have to wait long before his fingers skimmed the valley between her breasts, then slowly down to her belly button. When he glided a finger between the band of her panties and her bare skin, she closed her eyes.

"Look at me, dollface," he said, his voice just above a whisper. His blue eyes deepened to midnight as he peered down at her. Audrey's legs trembled. He pulled her onto the settee with him, straddling his thighs. The muscles of his belly rippled as he positioned her over his zipper. He slid his hands around her hips, moving her this way and that until the ridge of his erection beneath the straining denim aligned with her sensitive core. She gasped, and dug her fingers into his shoulders.

"Feel good?" he said.

"Mm, yes," she moaned.

He slipped his hands beneath the leg openings of her panties to cup her behind, then pulled her tighter against him. "Come on, baby," he coaxed, his voice throaty.

Her lace panties dampened, and he hadn't even touched her. Her sex ached with pent-up need.

Should she be brazen and bold? Or predictable and humdrum?

She closed her eyes, fighting the two sides of her personality. When he licked the swell of her breast, her body jerked. His fingers dug into the fleshy part of her bottom, holding her in place and rocking her oh-so-gently against his groin. Her skin burned hot beneath his touch. Sweet sensations radiated from her center, urging her to cross over to the dark side.

She braced her hands on the back of the settee, her arms on either side of his head. Her fingers curled around the top edge of the seat. "I need—" she panted.

"I know you do, baby."

Her knees squeezed his hips as she grazed her sex across the rough denim beneath her. Passion curled her toes. She began moving against him, aware he watched her through heavy lids.

"Come for me." He kissed her arm.

"Yes," she whimpered. When he nipped the tender skin above her breast, the dam burst. Her neck arched, and she cried out in release. Her fingers vise-gripped the settee as the shudders wracked her body. She collapsed onto his chest, and his arms wrapped around her.

"Good?" he asked, skimming his hands up and down her back through the satin robe.

"Mm, yes."

He shifted and pulled her sideways into his lap. He angled his head for a kiss, then paused. "What's this?"

She followed the downward direction of his gaze, thinking for a moment he was being a jokester again, that he referred to the evidence of his obvious arousal. What she saw resting in his upturned palm pulled the plug on her afterglow.

"Oh, God," she whispered. "That's my boob."

CHAPTER 4

Audrey didn't know whether to laugh or to cry. Dropping a fake boob in Zach's hand after what had just happened between them ranked in the top five most embarrassing moments of her life. Maybe even top two.

A sign, if ever there was one.

Grabbing the rubbery orb, she said, "I think I'll go now." She avoided his gaze as she climbed off his lap, wishing she could click her heels together three times and disappear.

His hand on her wrist stopped her. "What's going on here?"

"I bought the gel breast enhancers instead of the gel bra. The clerk at the lingerie store told me it was the wrong choice, but I didn't listen." She forced herself to look at him, to push all her mortification aside for the moment. "Zachary, I'm sorry. I should have told you the truth before…before we, um…" She curled her fingers around the fake breast, amazed how lifelike it felt in her hands.

Alcohol and orgasm fuzzed her head. Her limbs tingled with warmth. Relief, of course, relief this ridiculous charade was finally over. She could go home now.

"Why would I care that you had your implants removed, Ava?"

Champagne bubbles burst in her throat and stomach, and she willed herself not to burp. *Ava*. He still thought she was Ava. The churning in her stomach had to be from guilt, not relief. "I, ah, well, I just thought…"

"Don't be embarrassed," he said.

She forced a weak smile, and reached for the champagne. "Want more?" When he shook his head, she downed it straight from the bottle in one big gulp.

She set the bottle down and turned away, then pulled the lapels of her robe together. Her fingers fumbled at the sash, and she couldn't get it to tie. She said a few choice words under her breath.

"Ava." She heard Zach rise from the settee, then he grasped her shoulders and turned her to face him. He pushed her hands aside, and tied the sash for her. "You okay?"

"Fine. Embarrassed, mortified and humiliated, too. But fine. Peachy. Dandy." She burped. "Jim Dandy."

"I think you've had enough to drink. We both know how you react to too much champagne."

How would he know how she acted with too much champagne? Oh. Ava. Duh.

"I think it's great you had them removed, although I'm surprised."

Think fast, Audrey told herself. "I, uh, had some problems with them." What would happen when he next saw Ava...the *real* Ava? With *real* fake boobs? She'd let Ava deal with that. Not her problem.

His bare pecs flexed as he raked his fingers through his thick black hair and stared past the railing into the darkness of Sun Valley and Ketchum. "What just happened here?" he asked.

Did he really have to rub it in? "I think it's obvious, don't you?"

"Actually, I don't think it's obvious at all."

"My boob fell out. What else is there to say?"

His booming laughter startled her. "When did you get so funny?"

"I can't say *I'm* finding the humor in any of this." But she couldn't help the smile that tugged on her mouth.

"I wasn't talking about your, ah—" He motioned

to the gel-filled breast in her hand. She shoved it behind her back. "I meant what just happened between us."

She blinked. "Oh. That." She cleared her throat. "Um, what about it?"

"You've never acted like that with me before."

Audrey had never acted like that with *anyone* before. But he referred to Ava, of course. Disappointment sliced through her. "I haven't?"

He shook his head, not breaking her gaze. "No, you haven't."

"Well, that's because..." *Because what, Audrey?* She lifted her chin. Her brain was somewhere behind all that booze. "That's because *you've* never acted like that with *me* before."

His eyes narrowed. "True," he said.

His words sank in. A thrilling little buzz hummed in the pit of her stomach that had nothing to do with the champagne. *He'd never kissed Ava like he just kissed her.*

But he was in love with Ava. Wasn't he? Warning bells warred with celebration in her head. Oh, crap. She'd listened to her raging hormones rather than her common sense, and she'd blown it.

She moaned and pressed her palms to her temples. None of this made any sense. And none of it mattered. She'd forgotten her whole purpose for being here. She chanced a look through the French doors to the giant bed, and her legs started to quiver. She needed to get out of here, pronto.

She grasped the railing for balance, and tried to sift through the fuzziness in her head. She would just have to tell the truth. "I need to throw up," she said.

Zach rushed to her side and grabbed her elbow, leading her inside toward his private bathroom.

She yanked her arm from his grip, and stumbled toward the hall door with legs that would have embarrassed Gumby. "No, I'll just go back to my room and sleep it off. And throw up. Not necessarily in that order."

****

The next morning, Zach sat alone in the dining room, nursing his second cup of strong coffee. He glanced at the grandfather clock at the opposite end of the table for the third time in as many minutes. Maybe he should go check on her.

He shifted in his chair, not quite ready to see her. His and Ava's relationship had always been superficial, their kissing nothing more than a pleasant pastime. Since hiring her as his lead flight attendant, he'd never looked twice at her. But last night on the balcony... Wow. She'd been amazing. Even now, just thinking about it, his body tightened. Being attracted to her sure would make this whole charade more believable. It could also complicate matters. He pressed his lips together.

The rest of his family milled into the room, giving him the evil eye.

"Nice ruckus last night, brother," Theresa said, sitting across from him. "Do you think your *girlfriend* could possibly have made any more noise?"

"Yes, actually. I'm quite certain she could have," he said, his good humor returning.

Theresa leaned toward him and whispered, "I know what you're doing. They'll never buy it."

"Don't be so sure."

Theresa studied him. "This is about Rachel, isn't it? You're still ticked off at what they did to you."

Hearing Rachel's name used to feel like a fist in the gut. Now, it was more like a knife in the back. And his parents had helped her turn the blade. "Don't read anything more into this than the obvious."

She leaned back in her chair. "You've never been able to lie to me, baby bro."

His mother took the seat beside him, and righted the fine china cup so Stoudt could pour her coffee. Staying with his family was like being at a luxury hotel, with every need anticipated. He liked taking care of himself, doing things his own way.

He glanced at his mom as she sipped her coffee. She loved him, and wanted what was best for him. Both his parents did. But sometimes they were overzealous in their attempts to control his life. Sometimes, they got parenthood and business confused. Rachel's beautiful face popped into his mind, and he frowned.

His mom touched his forearm, and cleared her throat in a way that warned him he was about to be reprimanded. "You might want to remind Ms. Divine that some of us need our beauty sleep, and that we'd appreciate it if she observed the family's bedtime."

Theresa stared at her lap, hiding a grin. He held back his own smile. "Absolutely. I'll be sure to tell her."

"Where is your, ah, fiancée, anyway?" asked Garrett, shaking out the linen napkin and spreading it onto his lap. The word 'fiancée' seemed to stick in his throat.

Zach didn't hold back the smile this time. "She had a bit too much to drink last night and—"

The double doors leading from the foyer slammed open. Everyone jerked in their seats and turned toward the sound.

Zach almost spit his coffee onto the tablecloth. Ava stood in the doorway, her eyes shaded with black cat-eye glasses, and her body squeezed into skin-tight white capris and a red leather bustier.

"Oh, God," she muttered, leaning against the doorframe as if it would offer her support. "I need a drink."

His mom straightened primly. "It's barely nine in the morning, Ms. Divine."

Ava nudged the glasses down her straight nose and peered at the clock. "Oh, right. I need two drinks, then."

Zach burst out laughing, then hid the gaffe with a not-so-subtle coughing fit. His mother patted him on the back as if he were still just a kid. From behind him, Stoudt coughed, too. No way could the Banister butler, the epitome of decorum and respect, be hiding laughter.

"I'm sorry, Ms. Divine, but the bar doesn't open until noon here." Garrett's voice dripped with derision.

She glanced at the clock. "It's nine now." She counted on her fingers. "Ten, eleven, twelve. That's three hours. I guess I can wait that long." Her gaze landed on Zach for the first time. "Love Muffin? How about if you's-a come over here and help Ava-wava to her chair? I'm feeling a bit dizzy."

Zach bit his lip and stood, scooting his chair away with the backs of his knees. He met Stoudt's gaze, and could've sworn he saw amusement. Zach circled the table, then slipped his arm around Ava's waist. "You're killing me," he whispered into her ear, glad the hot episode between them last night hadn't affected her willingness to play the game.

"I'm sorry, Love Muffin," she said in a whisper loud enough for everyone to hear. "But it's your fault I'm in this condition. We're engaged now. You don't need to get me drunk to take advantage of me anymore." She giggled, then groaned loudly, pressing fingers to her temples.

Zach practically lost his hold on her.

He glanced around the table. His mother didn't look at them. Theresa stared out the window. Her husband stirred his coffee, his expression blank, and Garrett's lips pressed so tightly together that Zach wanted to warn him to watch his blood pressure.

After seating Ava beside him, Zach turned to Stoudt. "Would you mind getting Ava some aspirin? I'm afraid she's going to have a whopper of a headache."

Before Stoudt could respond, Zach heard the

unmistakable sound of pills rattling in a plastic bottle. He turned to see Ava pouring a whole bottle of aspirin into her mouth.

"Ava!" He grabbed the bottle from her hands. Her brows lifted behind her dark glasses. "Let's not get carried away," he muttered. "You're going to make yourself sick."

He could have sworn she batted her eyelashes before reaching for her water and taking a long drink. He half expected her to choke on all the pills, but she didn't.

"I wouldn't worry about it, brother," Theresa deadpanned from across the table. "She'll be throwing up after breakfast anyway." She turned to Ava. "Isn't that what models do to stay thin?"

Ava's head whipped up, and she drummed her fingers on the tablecloth. Finally, she said, "That, and a whole lotta sex."

Zach choked on his coffee, unable to save the tablecloth.

****

Audrey collapsed on the bed, fists pumping in the air, convinced her performance at breakfast had done the trick. Zach certainly wouldn't be in a hurry to marry a hung-over, pill-popping hussy.

"Ava baby, I'm coming home," she muttered, kicking her feet with glee.

She couldn't wait to leave Sun Valley, to leave Zach. Clearly, she had no self-control around him. She'd had every intention of breaking up with him last night. Instead, she'd come on his lap.

The knock on the door brought back her smile. That would be Zach.

Forcing the jubilant grin from her face, she took on her Ava persona for what should be the very last time. She slipped her feet into stiletto sandals before swinging open the door.

Zach whooped and swept his arms around her, then lifted her off the ground and swung her in a circle. He kicked the door shut and set her down. "Dollface, that was a riot. I almost pissed my pants, it was so good."

She sat on the edge of the bed. "Are you psychotic? I just made a complete boob of myself—"

"Pardon the pun." He grinned.

She glared at him. "Which should have made you furious, or at the very least embarrassed you, and you're smiling like the Cheshire Cat."

"I'm afraid I'm not following you." The amusement faded from his face, replaced with a look of concern and puzzlement.

Great! He was psychotic *and* dense. "I can't marry you, Zachary." Whew. There, she'd said it. She wanted to wipe her brow in relief.

"What?"

She glanced away, questioning again her sister's sanity. He was absolute ambrosia for the eyes. She slipped the engagement ring from her finger. "Look, Zachary. I think you're a really nice man, and we obviously have a good time together, but I just don't love you and don't want to marry you." Good. She couldn't be more blunt than that. She waited for his outburst.

When he didn't say anything, she turned to see his reaction. Zach bent forward, his face resting in his hands, and his shoulders shook.

Oh, God. She rushed over to him. "I'm so sorry." She reached out and touched his shoulder. "Don't be upset."

Zach whipped upright and grabbed her face, and gave her a big, smacking kiss before releasing her. When he pulled back, his laughter echoed between them.

"My God, Ava. You are priceless."

She stepped backward. "I don't understand you."

He motioned with his hands. "This is too much. Dollface, I think we have ourselves a little misunderstanding."

Her ears buzzed a warning. "In what way?" Did she really want the answer?

"Do you remember our phone conversation last week, when I invited you up here for the weekend?"

She blinked. Then blinked again. "Ah, of course I remember."

"What was my reason for asking you here?"

"You wanted me to meet your family."

He nodded. "And?"

Audrey scanned her memory for everything Ava had told her about her conversation with Zach. The "F" word! "You mentioned the word 'fiancée.'"

"And?"

"Why don't you just tell me where you're going with this?" She fisted her hands at her sides, the prongs of the ring digging into her palm.

"Remember me telling you how, when Theresa and I were in high school and college, we'd bring dates home we knew our parents would hate? And how they often tried to set us up on dates with people *they* thought were perfect for us?"

Dizziness enveloped her as comprehension crept into her mind.

"Recently, my parents took their matchmaking scheme too far." A shadow crossed his face, and he looked away for a moment. "I thought it was time to break out the game again, by bringing home a woman completely wrong for them. Any of this ringing a bell?"

Understanding sunk into Audrey's pores, and her stomach roiled. "You wanted a fake fiancée." She squeezed the ring in her hand.

He nodded, and his expression changed from amused to somber. "Ava, I—"

She held up her hand to stop his words, then turned away.

"I'm sorry," he said. "I thought you understood. On the phone, you—"

She turned back around. "So you have no

interest in marrying me?"

His apologetic gaze bore into hers. "None. I'm sorry."

"And the fun we had last night wasn't because you love me?"

He shook his head, and relief flooded through her. Thank God, she hadn't broken his heart. Ava had panicked over nothing.

"Whew!" She threw herself backward on the bed, arms overhead, her red leather bustier riding up her torso.

"Don't act so upset," he deadpanned.

She rose on one elbow. "Nothing personal, Zachary, but I don't want to marry you, either. Do you realize the lengths I've gone to, trying to convince you to break up with me? I broke into the kitchen last night, for goodness' sake. I stole some dry beans to put into the aspirin bottle. Those beans are probably expanding in my stomach as we speak."

He cocked his head. "You wanted to force me to break up with you?"

She nodded. "I didn't want to hurt your feelings."

He held up a hand and chuckled. "You've outdone yourself."

She sat up, drawing her knees beneath her. She lowered her gaze, and a blush heated her face. "If you wanted to marry Av—ah, me—as I thought, then I figured you must really care about me. I wanted to let you down gently."

He nodded once, then sat down beside her, his fingers curling over the edge of the mattress. "You are full of surprises, Ava Divine."

"You have no idea," she muttered.

Their gazes caught, and again her insides tugged. Too bad he thought she was someone else.

"Last night really messed me up," she said. "I shouldn't have gotten so carried away, since I was planning on breaking up with you." Her skin burned hotter. She resisted covering her face with her hands.

"So last night...was all part of *your* plan," he said, his voice light, like he didn't care either way.

"No! I didn't expect that to happen." She glanced at him from beneath her lashes. "But I'm glad it did. Well, except for the boob part." She giggled and held out her hand, uncurling her fingers from around the engagement ring. "Guess I won't need this anymore."

He returned her smile and stood. "How would you like to wear that for a couple more days, now that you know my heart's not pining for you?"

She chewed on her lower lip at the unwarranted hurt, then pushed the feeling aside. "So your sister is in on this? She knows we're not really engaged?"

"She suspects I'm up to my old tricks, yes. Don't expect any help from her, though—she thinks we'll never convince them."

She grinned and slipped his ring back onto her finger. "I think she's going to be eating her words, Mr. Banister."

CHAPTER 5

"I could strangle you right now, Ava," Audrey hissed into the cell phone.

"What did I do?"

"It's what you *didn't* do. What you didn't tell me." Audrey paced to the windows and peered out at the empty pool.

"What are you talking about?"

"Hmm, let's see. Where should I start? Oh, yes. How about, Zachary Banister never wanted to marry you."

"What!"

"Yep. And how about, this weekend is all just a joke to get even with his family. You send me here to do something that was your responsibility, and I make a total boob of myself, all because you weren't listening." Speaking of, she self-consciously adjusted her falsies, closing her eyes to make last night's memory disappear. When Ava didn't respond, Audrey said, "Well? Don't you have anything to say to me?"

"Some guy named Rod left you a message. Who is he? He sounds cute."

"I was thinking more along the lines of 'I'm sorry, Audrey.' Or 'How silly of me, Audrey.' Or 'Thanks so much for everything, Audrey. You always come through for me.'"

She waited.

Finally, Ava said, "Okay. Sure. Those things. So who's Rod?"

"He's a neighbor, and the principal at my school."

"Isn't that unethical?"

"We're not dating."

"Why? Is he ugly, bald, or fat?"

"None of the above. I'm just not sure I want to get involved with him."

There was a pause on the line. "You need to lighten up, Aud. Stop looking for Mr. Perfect, and be happy with Mr. Right Now."

"I should take romantic advice from *you*? She whose entire love life has been a procession of Mr. Right Nows?" Audrey paced back across the room, trailing her fingers along the footboard of the bed. She stopped under her buddy, the deer head.

Audrey *wanted* to meet Mr. Right, someone she could picture herself with in fifty years. Even though she'd recently turned thirty, desperation didn't define her yet. Just hope.

"Down! Down, dog. Audrey, your dog's breath really stinks. Do they make doggie breath mints? When did you say you're coming home?"

"I'm staying through the weekend as planned."

"What? Why?"

"Because you promised Zach you'd help him."

"I promised him no such thing."

"Maybe you don't remember, just as you don't remember other things about that conversation, but you did promise him, Ava. And because we Thompsons are girls of our word, I'm going to stay. Besides, like you've been telling me for years, I need some excitement in my life. Here's my chance."

"Well, be careful okay? I've known Zach Banister for a long time. I've seen the effect he has on women. I don't want you getting any stupid ideas."

"Gee. Thanks." She glanced up at the deer head. "Don't look at me like that," she muttered to her taxidermied friend.

"I don't mean it in a negative way, Aud. But I've seen the type of women he's dated. He dates women like *me*. *You* live in a small town, grow your own vegetables, stay home at night, and sit on your front porch watching sunsets..."

"I think we're getting ahead of ourselves here, sis. I'm not planning on falling in love with the man."

"What did he say when you told him who you really were?"

Audrey's face warmed. "He didn't say anything."

"He wasn't, like, totally shocked and ticked off?"

The deer head stared at her, silent. She headed back to the windows. "I haven't actually told him yet."

"What? Why not?" Ava shrilled.

Audrey pulled the phone away from her ear. "That would just complicate everything," she said toward the receiver. After a moment, she brought the phone back to her ear. "It was Ava Divine he invited here, so it should be Ava Divine who rides out the weekend."

But it would be Audrey Thompson's head on the wall if she screwed up.

****

Zach glanced up at Ava's balcony. She was supposed to join him at the pool. He couldn't wait to see what she had up her sleeve this time.

Having a fiancée, especially a *phony* fiancée, was much more fun than he expected. He still couldn't believe she thought he'd been serious about wanting to marry her, how she'd said "yes" just to spare his feelings.

Stretching his bare legs on the chaise lounge, he pulled the baseball cap over his face and closed his eyes, thinking about last night with her. For all the years he'd known her, he'd never kissed her like that. He'd never wanted to.

Maybe he'd never really tried to get to know her. Despite her outrageous exterior, he sensed a realness and vulnerability inside her that he'd never noticed before.

"Holy Christ," Garrett Banister muttered from

across the pool.

Zach nudged up his cap to see what had caused his father's quiet but forceful outburst. His jaw dropped.

Ava Divine and her body had arrived. She stood beside the pool deck, her gorgeous figure barely covered in a candy-apple red bikini. Her luscious breasts looked ready to fall out of the tiny scraps of material, and Zach's palms began to sweat. Her blond-streaked hair hung loose around her shoulders in an artfully messy tangle like she'd been making love all morning. Black cat-eye sunglasses shielded her eyes from the bright mountain sun.

Swallowing back a lump the size of Bald Mountain from his throat, Zach shifted in his chair to hide his growing interest in Miss Divine's amazing assets.

"Hi, Love Muffin!" she called, blowing him a kiss. "Wanna see something really incredible?"

Oh, yeah. Did he ever. "Sure thing, baby," he called back, his voice squawking.

She glided across the deck toward the deep end, her hips swaying with every step. She removed her sunglasses and set them on a nearby lounge. Did she plan to do a strip tease for him? Liquid fire shot straight to his groin. But here? In front of his entire family? No.

She surprised him by starting up the ladder of the high dive. "Are you watching?" she called from the fifteen-foot platform.

"Can't take my eyes off you," he said, his gaze glued to her shapely backside, which flexed and wiggled with every slow step up that ladder.

Could he possibly be more turned on? He imagined those long, toned legs wrapped around his hips as he buried himself deep inside her. Yeah. He could.

He pulled the cap from his head and set it on his lap, hiding his arousal.

She walked to the front of the diving board, the lines of her body fluid and lithe. He sensed the gazes of everyone present fixed on her as well.

Balancing on the edge by her toes, she gave a little jump in the air, raising her arms overhead like a ballerina. Then she leapt from the springboard. Just as Zach imagined a perfectly executed dive, she shouted, "Cannon ball!" tucked her legs into her chest, and landed in the water with a splash that soaked everyone on the perimeter.

Amidst the outraged sputtering from his family, Zach found himself smiling ear to ear. He rose from the lounge and headed to the edge of the pool. Her body moved through the deep water, and she emerged like a mermaid right in front of him, her hair slicked back and dark with water, her skin glistening like dew in the morning sun.

Squatting, he reached down to help her out. Instead, she tugged him into the water and pressed her near-naked body against his. His body reacted despite the mental reminder that this wasn't for real. For either of them.

Wrapping her arms about his neck, she pulled his face closer. Just when he expected to feel her soft mouth upon his, she whispered, "I lost my boob."

Zach choked back a laugh. "Excuse me?"

"My fake boob slipped out of my top, and is somewhere at the bottom of your pool," she muttered, then nibbled on his earlobe.

"How did that happen?" he asked, running his hands up and down her bare back, feeling goose bumps rise on her skin. From his touch, or the cool water?

She raked her fingers through his hair, and peered deep into his eyes. "There's a little pocket inside the bikini top that's supposed to keep it secure." She kissed a path to his ear. "Will you dive down and get it for me while I stay against the side here? Pretty please?" She batted her long eyelashes.

From this close proximity, he saw they were real.

"You're beautiful," he said before he could edit his thoughts.

Her face turned a flattering shade of pink, and she dropped her gaze. "My boob, please, before someone sees it down there." She made a motion with her head to the right. Theresa's husband stood and stretched in his Speedo, looking like he intended to dive in next.

Before he could stop himself, Zach planted a big kiss on her full mouth. She tasted of sunshine and promises. Pulling back, he said, "I'll be right back, dollface." He dove beneath the surface of the water, its coolness doing little to quench the inferno raging through his body.

****

Careful to stay against the side of the pool, Audrey moved into the shallow end until her feet touched bottom, and waited for Zach. When she'd pressed her bikini-clad body against his half-naked form—his *magnificent* half-naked form—she'd felt his erection against her lower belly.

A thrill shot upward from her toes, spreading through her body and warming her despite the cool water lapping at her skin. She'd never had so much fun.

Zach dove under for the second time, the water glistening off his wide shoulders in the mountain sun before he disappeared beneath the azure surface again. This time, he was successful, coming up for air right in front of her and giving her a knowing wink a split second before Speedo Man did a practiced dive into the deep end.

"My hero," Audrey murmured. She smiled as Zach stepped closer. Droplets of water glided down his chest, and pooled in his belly button before dripping lower to disappear into the band of his blue swim trunks.

"My lady," he said, pushing his hand toward her.

She reached for the boob as he moved to shield her from the family members who clearly weren't minding their own business. "Okay," she said, peering over his shoulder, "your family on the deck can't see what I'm doing, but Speedo Gonzales over there has a clear view."

Theresa's husband stood beside the pool, knocking the water from his ears and pretending not to watch them.

Audrey bit her lip. *Think like Ava,* she reminded herself. "If *you* put it back for me, then everyone will just think you're feeling me up." Butterflies on steroids raced through her belly.

Zach's mouth twitched at the corner, and Audrey had the urge to kiss him there again. But she held back. This was just a game. All games came to an end eventually.

"Okay, twist my arm," he muttered. "Slide your hands around my waist, and pretend I'm really turning you on."

"Like that will be hard," she whispered, doing as he said. His back muscles tensed under her touch as she raked her fake fingernails along his shoulder blades. He shivered. She ran her hands down his sides, stopping just shy of his waist band. Did his breathing just catch? She smiled inside.

His hand approached her breast, and she arched her neck and gave a dramatic moan of ecstasy. She bit her lip as his fingers dipped inside her bikini top, holding the material away with one hand while the other pushed the fake boob into its pocket.

As he removed his hand, his fingers brushed her nipple and it immediately pebbled, despite the innocent nature of his touch. A shot of pure desire leapt through Audrey's veins, and her wide-eyed gaze met his.

"Oops, sorry," he said. But he didn't look sorry, nor did he pull his hand away.

"It's okay," she whispered, and willed him with

her eyes to touch her there again.

As if he'd heard her unspoken plea, he covered her breast with his large hand and squeezed gently, all the while not breaking her gaze. His thumb flicked over her nipple, and Audrey quivered in his embrace.

She looked down, expecting to be embarrassed at the sight of his hand inside her bikini top. Audrey Thompson would have been. But the sight ignited a gentle but persistent throbbing between her legs.

"I can't stop thinking about last night." His husky voice whispered against her temple. His hand traveled to the curve of her hip, holding her close.

She looked up and met his intense gaze. "Really?" Her voice came out breathlessly.

He rolled her already aching nipple between his fingers and squeezed hard. She bit her lip to keep from crying out. "Really," he said.

He caressed and kneaded her breast while his other hand pressed their hips together. The hard ridge of his erection made her want to wrap her legs around his waist, lay back on the pool deck, and beg him to take her now.

But that would be taking the game too far. Wouldn't it?

"Oh for chrissake, get a room," Theresa called from the pool deck.

Zach gave Audrey a lopsided grin and removed his hand. She quickly adjusted herself, and found everything back in place. She cleared her throat. "Ah, thank you."

"Anytime," he said. His blue eyes deepened in color as he peered down at her. "I mean that."

She wiped pool water from her eyes and took his hand, letting him lead her from the water and feeling pretty much naked in this itsy bitsy bikini that barely had enough material to be legal. How could Ava wear this and feel...normal?

Pool water slid off her skin as she climbed the

steps out of the shallow end. Still holding Zach's hand, she followed him around the deck, then retrieved her glasses. After shading her eyes, she announced, "Excuse us, everyone. We're going to go have sex now."

Zach exploded into a coughing fit.

Audrey Thompson would never in a million years say something like that. She would also never in a million years *do* what her Ava-self had just proposed. She just wasn't that kind of girl.

Too bad. Playing naughty was damn fun.

CHAPTER 6

Zach tugged her into the house through the back door.

Inside the enormous laundry room, the washer and dryer hummed with a quiet drone, unlike her machines at home, which shook the whole house when in use.

Safe from the eyes and ears of his family, she let go of his hand and burst into giggles. She pushed her sunglasses to the top of her head. "I almost wet my pants out there. That was so much fun."

He slid the towel from around his neck and looped it around hers, tugging until their half-naked bodies were just inches apart. He wasn't smiling. Despite the heat from his body, goose bumps rose on her skin.

His dark gaze bored into hers. "You had a good idea out there." He pulled her closer until their hips touched.

She blinked. "Wh-What was that?" She couldn't think straight with his arousal pressing against her flesh. If her nipples got any harder, they'd pop the gel falsies right out of the bikini top.

"About having sex."

Excitement rippled her skin, and desire pooled between her legs. "I was, um, just playing the game."

He leaned toward her until his coarse chest hairs tickled the sensitive swell of her breasts. "It's my favorite game," he whispered.

Warning bells clashed with the hallelujahs in her head. She couldn't have sex with him. He thought she was someone else.

"I forgot my towel outside," she said, her voice

cracking.

"You can get another one."

"We're dripping water all over the floor."

"It'll wipe up." He kissed the side of her neck. Her knees almost buckled. She splayed her fingers on his chest, and his heart beat strong beneath her palms. *Push him away, Audrey.*

"Wanna play?" he asked, and the hot tip of his tongue dipped into her ear. She shivered.

No. She barely knew him. It would be wrong, because he thought she was Ava.

He thought she was Ava. To him, she *was* Ava. If she was supposed to be Ava, she should act like Ava. What would her sister do? Audrey's pulse roared in her ears.

His fingers tipped her chin so he could stare into her eyes. His steamy expression halted her breath and melted her resistance. Her lips slowly stretched into a grin.

"Roll the dice, big guy," she murmured in her sexiest voice.

His throaty chuckle reverberated against her chest as he backed her up against the whirring dryer. He lifted her onto the waist-high appliance. Warm, dry metal heated her bottom and thighs.

"You've got a great mouth, dollface," he murmured as he leaned in to kiss her. His hands slid down to cup her hips, pulling her close and positioning himself between her knees.

She wrapped her arms around his neck and returned the kiss. He tasted of iced tea and lemon. His tongue was hot, his hands hotter. The vibrations of the dryer competed with the throbbing between her legs. "Shouldn't we go somewhere more private?" she asked against his mouth, breathless already.

"No." He wrapped a forearm around her waist, and arched her backward to trail kisses down her neck and onto her breasts. He pushed the flimsy bikini top and a fake boob aside. "I like them real like this, baby."

He liked her breasts! "But someone might—" She gasped as he licked her nipple. "Someone might see us."

He laved his tongue around the aching peak. "That's what makes it so fun. Live on the edge, dollface."

Live on the edge. How many times had Ava told her just that? How many times had she told herself that? How many times had she ignored the advice?

She tangled her fingers in his hair and pulled his head closer. He cupped the underside of her breast and lifted it for greater access. He suckled her, and she yelped softly at the pleasure and pain of his teeth on the sensitive peak.

Her body's reaction shocked and thrilled her as she wriggled closer to him. His mouth left her breast with a soft popping sound as the suction released. He met her gaze briefly before dropping to his knees. When he grasped her legs and hooked them over his shoulders, she realized his intention.

"Oh, no."

"You want me to stop?" he asked, his voice deep and husky.

The good girl side of her certainly did. Good girls got to know a man before letting him get so intimate. But the bad girl side wanted this, *yearned* for this. Zach kissed the inside of her knee, sending shivers rippling across her skin. Oh, who was she kidding?

Her lips tugged into a grin. "No, I don't want you to stop."

He returned her smile with a rakish one of his own. He caressed her thighs and hips before pulling off the string bikini bottom.

Any self-consciousness took flight when he leaned in and kissed the triangle of hair between her legs. She closed her eyes. His hot breath scorched her skin. When his tongue touched her, her body jerked involuntarily. A moan escaped her parted lips. She curved her fingers around the dryer's front edge, wanting, needing more of his touch.

"Mmm." She sighed and speared his hair with her fingers, pulling his head closer. He slipped a finger between her folds, teasing, touching, not quite entering her.

"Zach, please," she begged.

His fingers thrust deep inside her, swirling and dipping and probing as the dryer trembled beneath her. When his teeth grazed her sensitive nub, Audrey saw stars.

"Mm, there. Oh! Yes!" she cried, riding the precipice of rapture. Her fists bunched in his thick, damp hair. The crescendo rose inside her, stronger and stronger. The dryer gave a final shudder, the buzzer sounding with the end of the cycle just as Audrey exploded from the inside out. Wave after wave of orgasm crashed against Zach's pleasuring mouth.

Finally, he pulled away. He kissed her inner thigh, then the inside of her knee before unhooking her legs from his shoulders. Audrey's legs dangled off the edge of the dryer, weak with spent passion. He picked up her bikini bottom from the tile floor, then rose to his full height.

"And the buzzer marks the end of the game," she said under her breath, stunned from the physical sensations roiling through her entire being.

He handed her the red scrap of material, and his fingers lingered on hers.

"What about you? When do you get to play?" she asked. She'd been so caught up in the feel of his hands and mouth upon her body, she hadn't had a chance to touch him. She curled and uncurled her fingers. What an amateur. Ava would be appalled.

He chuckled and lifted her off the dryer. "It didn't occur to me to bring a condom to the pool this afternoon."

She couldn't help laughing with him as she

pulled on her suit. "Well, there's always next time."

His gaze turned serious for a moment, then his smile returned. "There is that."

He reached for his fallen towel and used it to wipe her from his mouth. She adjusted the ties on her bikini bottom, needing the distraction to settle her unease.

"Oh! I beg your pardon," came a deep British voice from the doorway.

Audrey looked up. Stoudt backed out of the room with a slight bow, his face cherry red. After he disappeared, she met Zach's gaze. They burst out laughing.

"Do you think he saw anything?"

Zach shrugged. "If he did, we'll never know. The man is nothing if not discreet."

Her heart raced. Zach was right. The threat of getting caught made it much more exciting. She wanted him again. Now.

"I need a shower." She nudged his shoulder. "Last one there's a rotten egg!" she cried, sprinting out of the room.

****

Zach raced after her with a startled laugh. She ran through the kitchen, and he followed. She ran through the foyer, right past Stoudt, and he followed, giving the older man a mock salute as he raced by. She scampered up the stairs, and he followed two steps at a time until he caught her at the top, yanking her into his arms and swallowing her shriek of laughter with his kiss.

Her sweet lips opened beneath his, kissing him back with answering fervor. She flung her arms around his neck and he half-dragged, half-carried her down the hall. He pulled her inside her room, kicking the door shut with his bare heel.

He ran his hands up and down her body, loving how she shuddered at every touch, like this was all new to her. Downstairs, he'd almost been convinced she was nervous. In all the time he'd known her, he'd barely given sex with her more than a passing thought. There had never been any chemistry.

But being with her now was thermal combustion. His body burned for her. He couldn't remember the last time he'd been so turned on.

He backed her toward the bed, but when they ran into the mattress, she muttered against his mouth, "Not here. Shower."

He caught her lower lip between his teeth. "The shower can wait."

She shook her head and pulled away. "But we've got eyes in here."

Zach jerked his head up and glanced around, expecting to see the maid or ever-present Stoudt standing in the corner, mouth agape. He saw nothing.

She motioned toward the fireplace and the deer head. "Bambi's watching."

He laughed, loving this funny side of her, and led her into the bathroom. The glass-enclosed shower took up an entire wall. He reached into the two-person stall, and turned on the water.

Despite having known her for several years, he'd never really *known* her until today. His body burned with desire. He couldn't wait to make love to her. She gave him a bashful glance through a thick fringe of black lashes, and he remembered she was just playing a game. He didn't care. As long as she played it with him.

She reached behind her neck and untied her bikini top. With a flick of her wrist, the red material floated to the floor.

He took his time devouring her with his eyes. Her smooth skin glowed with just a touch of sun. The damp ends of her tangled hair curled over her shoulders. One lock coiled perfectly around a rosy nipple. He traced his finger around it. She caught her breath and closed her eyes.

With one step, he erased the space between them and planted a long, leisurely kiss upon her upturned mouth. Her hands flattened against his chest, pushing him away. She gave him a sly smile, and leaned in to kiss his collarbone. Then she laved her tongue across one of his flat nipples. Almost painful desire rippled across his skin, and he grew even harder. She moved lower still, and circled her tongue in and around his belly button. As she dropped to her knees, she hooked her red-tipped fingers in his trunks, then slid them over his buttocks to the floor where he stepped out of them. His erection sprang free.

"Your turn," she said.

Audrey stared at his beautiful, naked body. Ambrosia for the eyes. A blush heated her face. She'd read enough sexy romance novels to know what she was supposed to do next, but reading, fantasizing, and actually *doing* were three completely different things. And she hadn't done *this* since college.

Be Ava, be Ava, be Ava.

She touched her tongue to him. He jerked. She took him into her mouth. He groaned and thrust his hands into her hair. His reaction delighted her, encouraged her. She swirled her tongue around the smooth head of his penis, and he shuddered.

Still, she sensed him holding back. She smiled around his erection, then wrapped her fingers around him and used her other hand to cup his sac as she took him in and out of her mouth. His fingers dug into her scalp, urging her closer. She used her teeth, her tongue, and her lips to coax tormented gasps from his mouth.

Finally, he pushed her away. "Dollface, you're killing me," he growled, hooking his hands under her arms and pulling her to her feet.

The bikini bottom stuck to her damp skin as he peeled it from her body. He motioned her into the hot spray of the shower. The water beat down on her hyper-sensitized skin, heating her body even more, as she heard him root around the medicine cabinet. He reappeared in the shower doorway and flashed a big grin, holding up something in his hand. "The bathrooms here are always fully stocked." He held a foil-wrapped disc between his index and middle fingers.

Thank God one of them was thinking clearly. "There are condoms in all the bathrooms?" Was that weird, or was it just her?

He stepped into the stall and wrapped his arms around her from behind, his large, wet hands cupping her breasts and teasing her nipples with his thumbs. "I learned that when I was a teenager. Came in handy more than once, I'll tell you."

A jealous shiver ran up her spine as he kissed and nipped at her shoulders. Her jealousy over women he'd been with in the past bordered on ridiculous. She focused on right now, right here.

Hot water sluiced across their skin, and his erection nudged her bottom. She poured a bead of liquid soap into her palms and lathered them with the thick foam, then reached behind her and took hold of his thick, heavy shaft. She felt and heard his sharp intake of breath as she squeezed and fondled him.

One of his hands slid down to her belly and into her pubic hair. His finger found her still-swollen clit, and she jumped. While he toyed with that sensitive nub, his other hand played with her breasts. Her nipples hardened until they almost hurt.

He turned her in his arms. After several kisses that sidelined her equilibrium, he directed her to the built-in seat at the far end of the two-person stall. His gaze held hers as he turned on the second shower head and lifted the nozzle from its perch. "Spread your legs," he commanded softly.

It didn't occur to Audrey not to obey. She

wanted whatever he offered.

She gasped as he aimed the hot spray between her legs, a direct hit upon her already-sensitive flesh. He knelt before her and captured her mouth for a long, deep kiss as he continued to caress her with pulsing water. Audrey couldn't think straight. She couldn't even kiss him back.

"Zach, I can't—"

"Yes, you can." He kissed behind her ear, then tugged her earlobe into his mouth.

"It's too much."

"No. Let it go, dollface."

She couldn't stand it anymore. She pushed at his chest, pushed at the hand holding the nozzle. Too much, too much, too—

He caught her scream of passion with his mouth as the climax lifted her off the seat. She was mid-orgasm as he picked her up and lowered her onto his massive erection. Her legs encircled his waist as her still-spasming vaginal walls clenched around him. He filled her and moaned his pleasure.

"Good Lord, you're tight," he groaned, pushing deeper into her. "So damn tight."

Dimly, she realized he'd put on the condom. How and when, she had no clue. His focus on pleasing her took her so far over the edge, she was practically incoherent with passion.

He pressed her against the wall, the cool tiles doing nothing to chill her ardor. She squeezed her thighs against his waist, and dug her fingers into his shoulders. He clutched her bottom, and lifted her up and down along his shaft. His groan rumbled against her mouth as his hips bucked into her over and over, the hard tiles bruising the thin skin over her spine.

The veins in Zach's neck strained as he pumped faster into her, his fingers digging into her flesh. Finally, he arched his neck and cried out his release into the pounding spray of hot water as he came inside her. She wrapped her arms around him, and held him as he buried his face in her shoulder.

After several long moments, he lifted her off his fading erection, and set her back on her feet. Audrey's legs trembled. As if sensing she needed his support, he enveloped her in a bear hug, and let the warm spray beat upon their sated bodies.

"Why the hell did it take us so long to do this?" he muttered against her neck.

"I just got here yesterday."

His warm breath tickled her ear as he chuckled. "I meant, if I'd known how much fun we'd have together, we would've done this years ago."

The funny little flip in her chest collided with the guilt over this charade.

"You were afraid of falling in love with me, that's why." She kept her voice light, then forced a grin.

He pulled away to stare into her face. Thankfully, he returned the smile. He gave her a smacking kiss on the mouth, then reached down to peel off the condom. After washing himself off, he stepped out of the shower and reached for a towel, then slung it low on his waist. She tried not to lick her lips as water beaded on his bare chest, dripping between his pecs, toward his belly button and lower.

"That's what's so great about you, Ava. We can just have fun together with no chance of either of us getting the wrong idea."

Ava. Big slap of reality. In his mind, he'd just had sex with Ava. Not Audrey. And he wanted nothing more from her than sex.

Well, of course he didn't.

He reached into the stall, and trailed his hand down her arm. "Later, dollface."

Audrey turned her face into the pounding spray, her fists clenched, needing the water to cleanse her disquiet. Her body might be sated, but her heart ached with misgivings. He was right about them having a good time together. He was right about how

Ava wanted no strings, no commitments. He was right about how Ava would never be stupid enough to fall for him.

But he was wrong about one thing.

She wasn't Ava.

****

The next morning, Audrey stood beside Zach as he loaded his golf clubs into the back of his Jeep.

"You didn't come down for breakfast," he said, watching her face.

Her skin burned. She couldn't tell him she'd laid awake half the night thinking about him. After the laundry room and the shower, she'd pretty much expected him to visit her bedroom after dinner. He hadn't. She kept forgetting the rules of this game. No commitment. No expectations. Just fun.

She shrugged and forced an Ava grin. "You wore me out yesterday. I overslept."

He studied her face a moment, and must have been satisfied by what he saw as he returned her smile. "You sure you don't want to come with me now to the golf course?"

She made a face. "I can do without all the opening ceremonies and evil looks from your dad and Allan. Besides, I still need to figure out the next part of our game."

"What's your plan?"

Her pasted-on grin faltered. "I have a few ideas up my sleeve."

"You're not wearing sleeves." His warm gaze traveled across her bare arms. She crossed them in front of her chest, squeezing herself some deeper cleavage with the help of the falsies. Zach cocked his head and stared openly.

She slapped his arm. "Stop that."

"After yesterday, can you blame me?" The desire in his eyes swept a burning blush up from her toes. He opened the Jeep door, propping one foot on the running board. "Have I told you lately how much I appreciate this?"

"You can tell me again, if you like."

He chuckled. "Seriously, you're making them crazy. Serves them right."

"For what, Zach? What's this really about?"

He slid his sunglasses farther up his nose. "It's just a practical joke, like I told you."

She swallowed back a lump of disappointment, and twisted her shoe into the aggregate driveway. "So what happens when they learn we're not really engaged?" *And what happens when you learn I'm not Ava?*

"They'll probably be very relieved." He cleared his throat. "So, you'll meet us down at the golf course?"

She nodded.

His grin returned. "God. I can't wait." He climbed into the Jeep, then pulled the door shut behind him. He leaned his left arm on the open window ledge. "Give me a kiss for good luck, dollface."

At least he hadn't called her "Ava." She braced her hands against the Jeep's door and leaned toward him, touching her lips to his. She started to pull back, but he hooked his fingers around her neck and drew her closer, the warm metal of the vehicle seeping through her thin cotton blouse. This might have been a game to him, but to her it was becoming far too real. His tongue swept inside her mouth, and she opened to him. She shoved her fingers into his wavy hair, bringing his face closer and holding him there until they both needed to come up for air.

"Good luck," she whispered, her voice throaty and soft—just like Ava's.

He started the Jeep, then peered at her from behind the black lenses. "I'll see you in a bit. Cheer loudly."

"Bet on it," she said.

Another day of pretending to be someone else.

Another day of Zach enjoying his time with "Ava," not her.

Yippee.

****

Zach waited his turn to tee off at the first hole of the golf course in Sun Valley. His brother-in-law, Allan, had a Sergio Garcia waggle going that made Zach want to shout, "Just hit the damn ball, already!"

His family had sponsored this one-day Memorial Weekend golf tournament for as long as Zach could remember. He enjoyed golf, and because it was for charity, he tried to make it every year, despite knowing his parents would probably have invited a woman or two to keep him company for the weekend. This year, Ava had saved him from that fate.

He glanced around. No Ava in sight. Yet. Just thinking about her sent his pulse speeding and his palms sweating.

Allan finally swung his club, shooting the ball straight down the fairway to land somewhere along the 250-yard mark. The sparse crowd clapped politely. Allan handed his club in the direction of his caddy, and smiled his practiced smile that told everyone, *I'm good, and you're not. I'm rich, and you're not. I'm invited to play at this tournament, and you're not.*

Zach still couldn't see what Theresa saw in the man. Growing up, his older sister had been such a romantic. Zach couldn't have been more shocked the first time he'd met Allan. His sister's choice seemed about as wrong as an Easter egg hunt in Iraq.

Theresa used to talk about how she couldn't wait to meet Mr. Right and fall madly in love. But somewhere along the way, her ideals had been replaced by those of their parents. The only thing Allan had going for him, as far as Zach could tell, was his uncanny ability to pick stocks. The man could be a Neanderthal in every other way, and it wouldn't matter to the Banisters. Maybe if Ava were a financial whiz, his family would embrace her—

What was he thinking? He didn't give a crap if his family approved of his choice of partner. If anything, he preferred they *dis*approve. Besides, Ava was his *temporary* girlfriend.

Pushing away the unsettling thoughts, he bent and placed his ball on the tee. Straightening, he adjusted his grip and gazed out over the fairway, planning his shot. A balmy breeze rippled through the cottonwood. Zach's gaze locked on a spot about 280 yards away. He shifted his footing, swung the club over his right shoulder, and—

"Go, Love Muffin, go!" Ava shrieked from the crowd.

—and Zach shanked the ball. The dimpled orb flew off at a right angle. The spectators ducked as the ball whizzed over their heads and thwacked a tree. By some stroke of luck, it stayed in bounds.

The crowd hummed with amusement. From behind him, Zach's father said, "What is *she* doing here?"

"I invited her, Dad, being that she's part of the family now."

Garrett's lips thinned. "Don't remind me."

"Who knows, maybe next year, she'll play with us."

Garrett's face drained of color, and he pushed Zach out of the way to take his shot. Zach turned his head to hide his grin.

As his father prepared to tee off, Zach waved at Ava. She looked fabulous and flamboyant as usual, in a flippy mini skirt and low-cut leather blouse that had her cleavage rising to new heights. If he didn't have first-hand knowledge of the little gel-filled sacks in her bra, he would never guess she'd had the implants removed.

He'd always been a fan of big breasts, but with Ava, he preferred the smaller size that fit perfectly in his hands. The thought of her breasts took some of the sting out of shanking the ball. Normally, he took his golf game seriously, especially when charity money was involved, but today he couldn't care less. So he'd lose a shot here. Big deal. He had more pleasurable things to ponder than a bad golf game. Like Ava's breasts. And her delectable body. And the soft little sounds of pleasure she made when he was kissing her, whether on the mouth or...

He shifted his stance, holding his club in front of his crotch. He was like a horny teenager with her. Just thinking about her got him hard.

"Quiet, please," the course marshal announced, and his voice seemed to be directed at Ava. She appeared nonplussed by the indirect censure. Zach wished he knew what was going through her head, and what she had in store for the rest of the game. Whatever it was, he couldn't wait.

Because of his horrible first shot, he bogied the first hole. Not bad, considering his wayward thoughts. Instead of visualizing his next shot, he visualized Ava's body. Her naked body. With her long, gorgeous legs wrapped around his waist as he plunged into her. He couldn't stop fantasizing about her. He purposefully hadn't gone to her room last night. Spending the night with a woman made it too real. Neither of them wanted that.

Ava joined the small group of spectators who followed Zach's foursome along the course. When she stepped off the paved path onto the grass by the second tee, her spiked heel sank into the soft turf.

Her little shriek turned the heads of everyone present—primarily the men, who'd been eyeing her nearly as often as Zach had been.

As if in slow motion, she tumbled forward and crumpled to the ground. In what reminded Zach of a slapstick comedy movie, male spectators rushed to her side before he had taken a single step.

Giving her "rescuers" a grateful smile, Ava let

them help her to her feet. "Oh, my goodness, that was clumsy of me. Thank you *so* much for your help," she told the gawking men, batting her eyelashes. She patted her hands up and down her torso as if to make sure everything was where it should be.

Did she not realize her every move hypnotized those idiots milling around her? She met Zach's gaze as he marched toward her, and she puckered her lips and blew him an air kiss. Yes. She knew *exactly* the effect she had on those men.

Zach reached her side as she brushed the grass from her skirt. He glared at the men, who seemed to have tunnel vision for her heaving cleavage, her legs, and her shapely rear. He wanted to punch each and every one of them. Usually, he didn't care if other men showed interest in his female companions.

But this—this felt an awful lot like jealousy. Not good.

"Are you okay?" he snapped, hating the confusion jerking him in three directions at once.

She placed her manicured hand on his forearm. "I'm fine." She lifted her foot and rotated it a few times. "Nothing broken."

"Those are the most ridiculous shoes to wear on a golf course."

She shot him a look of exasperation. "Stilettos are a girl's best friend."

"You could have broken an ankle."

"Thanks, Dad."

He gripped her upper arms, and turned her to face him. "I'm serious, Ava. You had all these guys rushing over to help you like a bunch of—of—" He couldn't think of a word pathetic enough to describe them.

"You sound jealous," she purred.

Dammit! "Don't be ridiculous. I need to get back to the game." He spun around and returned to his foursome.

She made kissy sounds behind him, but he didn't look back, because if he did he knew he'd see her luscious lips pursed in his direction. Then he'd picture those luscious lips pursed around something else—

No way. If he thought his game was distracted now...

The breeze picked up by the time Zach's group reached the second green. A gust of wind hissed through the trees, and clouds rolled through the bright blue sky. *Great.* His game sucked enough today.

As he waited his turn to putt, the tinkling strains of striptease music reached his ears.

Oh, God.

"She brought her blasted cell phone?" Allan asked, loud enough for everyone to hear.

Zach bit back a grin, and tried to look as irritated as the rest of the group. "I'll talk to her," he offered, and strode across the green.

"Oh, absolutely, Alfie," she said into the phone as he approached, apparently clueless to all the dagger-filled stares directed at her. She wriggled her fingers at him and mouthed, "Just a sec," with those candy-apple red lips.

Zach's father stepped between them. "That is quite enough, young lady," he said, grabbing the phone from her fingers. He shut it with an audible *snap*. A few of the nearby spectators clapped politely, as if they'd just witnessed an admirable golf shot.

Ava slapped her hands on her hips. "That was my plastic surgeon you just hung up on, buster!"

"I don't care if it was the President of the United States," Garrett said. "There are certain rules of etiquette a person must follow when on a golf course, and you, Miss Divine, have managed to break every single one of them with sixteen holes to go."

"Rules?" she asked, and Zach could have sworn she batted her eyelashes.

Garrett's grip tightened on his club, as if he wished to whack her with it. "A dress code, for one."

She fingered her low-cut blouse. "I'm wearing a collar."

Zach hid his burst of laughter behind a cough, and tried to look annoyed for his father's benefit.

"You are trying my patience," Garrett muttered.

Ava peered up at his father with her big green eyes. "Whoops. My bad," she muttered in a throaty, sexy voice. "I promise to behave myself from here on out." Her eyelids fluttered some more.

Garrett's face turned beet red, and he stumbled back a step. Zach couldn't contain his laughter this time. His dad glared at him.

Turning back to Ava, Garrett said, "I don't think you would know how to behave yourself." He snapped his fingers over her head. "Marshal!" The course marshal scurried over. "Please escort Miss Divine back to the clubhouse, where she can await our return." He marched away as if that were that.

"Oooh, I just *love* a man in control," Ava cooed after him as the marshal took her arm. She met Zach's gaze. "That's why I love you, Zachy-poo." She blew him a kiss, then finger waved "bye-bye" to the group.

Zach was probably the only one sorry to see her go.

CHAPTER 7

Audrey glanced around the lavish Banister garden, making sure she was alone before slipping off her high heels to walk barefoot in the soft, green grass. The yard smelled and looked recently mowed.

"Ah, heaven," she murmured, raising her face to the late-afternoon sunshine. Birds chirped from surrounding trees and bees hummed in the nearby rose bushes.

After being relegated to the clubhouse at the golf course, she'd soon grown bored, and asked the Banister driver to give her a ride back to the house. Thinking of the spectacle she'd made of herself at the tournament, she grinned. She supposed she should be concerned she was having such fun being naughty, but darn it all, she'd spent a lifetime being a good girl. She deserved a few days of kicking up her heels, especially when forced to wear these horrid, uncomfortable stilettos.

A girl could do worse than having to laze away a sunny summer afternoon at a Sun Valley mansion, she mused, entering a beautiful weathered gazebo.

When she'd first met Zach, she'd figured him as pretentious as these surroundings...just like the rest of his family. But he fit in with the Banister clan about as well as she did. He was down-to-earth, and had a terrific sense of humor. Never mind what he could do to her body. Her breath quickened just thinking about all the places he'd touched her.

She sighed. In a couple of days, she'd return to Boise and her safe, predictable life. She stared at the diamond on her ring finger. On a long, wistful breath, she let herself imagine what it would be like if her relationship with him were real.

The fantasy lasted about a millisecond, and she straightened on the bench with a frown. Wealthy and jet-setting Zachary Banister would never in a million years be interested in conservative and middle-class Audrey Thompson.

She stretched her legs out in front of her. She supposed she'd just enjoy the game while it lasted. Maybe she'd learn a thing or two to take back to her life in Boise.

"Having fun?"

Audrey's eyes flew open as Theresa stepped into the gazebo.

"You scared me. I didn't hear you come up." She scooted over on the bench to make room. "Yes, it's beautiful out here," she said.

Theresa sat down. "I meant, are you having fun with Zach's little game?"

Audrey hid her bare feet in the shadows, remembering Ava's advice never to be caught without the stilettos. "I can't believe anyone is buying it, but yeah. I'm having a good time." She smiled.

Theresa didn't quite return the smile. "It's hard not to buy it with the way you two are carrying on."

Audrey's skin burned. She cleared her throat.

"Zach and I used to do this to our parents when we were teenagers," Theresa said, placing her hands behind her on the bench and circling her head around a few times as if she had a kink in her neck. She laughed. "I could never outdo him, did he tell you that?"

Audrey shook her head.

"He always knew exactly the type of girl to bring home who would get under our parents' skin. I swear, that boy should have been an actor. He really knows how to play the doting boyfriend."

Audrey focused on the leaves of the quaking aspen across the garden. "Is this where you're going to warn me not to get too caught up in the game, to not fall in love with him?"

Theresa looked at her. "No matter how upfront he was with the girls, they always got the wrong idea."

Audrey forced a chuckle. "Don't worry. I'm about as interested in a serious relationship as he is." Which was true, if she referred to Ava.

Theresa cocked her head and pursed her lips. "Uh-huh. I've seen the way you look at him."

"He's easy on the eyes, in case you hadn't noticed." Audrey kept her tone light. "Don't forget what I do for a living, Theresa."

"Ah, yes. I do remember. So you're really an actress? That wasn't just part of the joke?"

Audrey shook her head. "My, ah, primary job is flight attendant in Zach's company."

"So Zach is your boss."

Audrey hadn't really thought about that.

"Aren't you afraid that this could damage your work relationship?"

"Why would it? Our relationship is no different now than it's ever been." Which was also completely true, if they referred to Ava.

Theresa plucked a petal from a red rose vine twining around the railing. "I've also seen the way my brother looks at you."

Audrey's pulse sped up. "Like you said, he's been doing this for years."

"Perhaps," Theresa said. She opened her mouth to say something more, but stood up instead. She nodded to the ring on Audrey's finger. "Just don't forget it's all pretend."

Audrey watched Theresa disappear into the maze of raised rock beds and roses, then leaned back into the railing. Did Theresa mean Zach's carefree façade was just that, a façade? Was he not as immune to this game as he appeared to be?

What would he do when he found out she wasn't

who she said she was?

****

Zach met Theresa coming out of the gardens. "Did you see Ava in there?"

"She's in the gazebo." She started to brush past him, and he grabbed her arm, halting her.

"What did you say to her?"

She laughed and pulled her arm free. "What? You're afraid I'm trying to sabotage your fun?"

"It wouldn't be the first time," he said dryly.

She patted his cheek. "Don't worry, little bro. Your secret's safe with me."

"Why do I get the feeling you're not telling me the whole story?"

She feigned indignation. "That hurts."

"Deal with it. What happened?"

"Just be careful. I have a feeling she's hiding something."

"You don't trust any woman I date."

"Neither do you, or you wouldn't still be bringing home fake girlfriends." She glided off with all the grace of the charm school graduate she was.

Damn!

He should be delighted Ava concerned even Theresa, who was in on the joke. But he hoped his sister had been nice to her. The Ava Divine he thought he knew could brush off any unfriendliness with the blink of a fake eyelash. But this new Ava...He had a feeling she wasn't so thick-skinned.

An empty gazebo greeted him. He knew Ava ⸻ gone back to the house because she would ⸻ him. Zach strode toward the river.

⸻ cottonwood and aspen, Ava ⸻ foot, her shoes dangling from ⸻ d in the shadows to admire ⸻ shone on her upswept hair, ⸻ tendrils around her face. The ⸻ ed her curvy hips and showed ⸻. She'd changed into a white gypsy shirt that hung low on one shoulder, revealing a creamy expanse of skin. His fingers tingled in anticipation, as if she'd bared that shoulder just for him. He'd always thought her beautiful, but now...

He recalled the intimacies they'd shared. The feel of her slick, wet body pressed against his in the shower; the way her nipples hardened with just the briefest touch of his fingers; her hot, tight sheath clamped around him. Everything about her—the sight, the feel, the taste of her—left him wanting more. His slacks tightened at the crotch.

He realized he also genuinely liked her company. He'd never had a woman friend. Plenty of female acquaintances. But one with whom he could horse around and be himself? Never. He hadn't trusted one enough for that.

Zach took a step toward her, and a twig crackled beneath his feet.

Ava turned toward him and smiled. "Hi," she said. "You're back earlier than I expected."

"Hi, yourself." His feet crunched on old leaves as he crossed the bank to stand beside her and stare out at the slow-moving water. "I didn't feel like hanging around for the closing ceremonies."

"How did you do?"

He shrugged. "I've played better. You okay?"

"Why wouldn't I be?"

He shoved his hands into his pockets and rocked back on his golf shoes. "You've had a busy day. You've been scolded by my father, kicked off the golf course, and accosted by my sister."

"Don't worry." She smiled, but it didn't reach her eyes. "I'm fine."

Zach pressed his fingers to his temples, reminding himself yet again that he should be gl[ad] their plan was working so well. But her feeli[ngs] were hurt. "How would you like to get out of he[re for] a while?" he asked.

Relief flooded her emerald eyes. "I w[ould]

that. I'm feeling kind of cooped up, which doesn't make a lot of sense, considering your family's estate is bigger than my neighborhood."

He tugged her toward the house. "Grab your purse, and meet me in the foyer in fifteen minutes."

"Where are we going?"

Where *were* they going? "Uh...We can head up to my cabin for the day. You might want to change into some jeans."

"Ava doesn't wear jeans," she said.

He grinned at how she referred to herself in third person, then wondered what had possessed him to invite her to his cabin. A woman who didn't wear jeans. She'd take one look at the remote and primitive surroundings, and demand he take her back to civilization.

Just like Rachel.

He worked the muscles in his jaw, biting back the bad memory. "If you hate it, I'll bring you right back."

"I won't hate it." One perfectly-arched eyebrow rose. "As long as there are no taxidermied animal heads inside."

He smiled, liking her more and more every minute.

****

Audrey brushed her teeth and touched up her makeup. Her stomach knotted at the thought of being alone with Zach at his cabin.

She'd pretty much been nuts from the time she'd agreed to this whole charade. Why stop now?

It would be nice to get away from the prying eyes of his family for a few hours. Never in her life had she experienced such disdain. She wondered if her sister experienced this reaction on a regular basis. She hoped not.

She still had a few minutes before Zach expected her downstairs. Picking up her cell phone, she speed-dialed her home number.

Her sister answered on the fourth ring, and she sounded out of breath. "Shoot me now."

Audrey tucked the phone between ear and shoulder as she swiped coral lipstick across her mouth. "Please tell me you didn't sell my dog."

"I hadn't thought of that, but no. I'm bored silly, sis. I can't believe you don't even have cable."

Audrey squinted at herself in the mirror. "I don't watch much TV." She tipped the ends of her lashes in black mascara. Audrey Thompson would never wear so much makeup to a cabin, but as Ava...She'd better add a second layer.

"What do you do for excitement around here?" Ava asked.

"I don't know, I hike the foothills, go to movies with my friends, work out."

"Oh. My. God. Audrey baby, you need to get a life."

Audrey stopped mid-lash with the mascara. "I like my life, thank you very much."

"Uh-huh. That's why you're still pretending to be me. How's it going?"

"Promise not to laugh, okay?"

"Shoot."

"I'm falling for Zach."

Ava didn't laugh. She didn't say anything for a long time. The mantle clock ticked, ticked, ticked in the silence. "What?" Her soft tone conveyed her disbelief.

"I know it's silly, because it's not really *me* he likes but *you*, but...I don't know. I'm feeling things around him I've never felt with anyone else."

Quiet echoed on the line. "Does he feel the same way about you?"

No, he feels the same way about you. Audrey rubbed a finger across her bottom lip as she inhaled a shaky breath. "Well, I took your advice and have been, ah, living it up a little."

"How 'little?'"

Audrey stared at her reflection, and saw Ava staring back at her. Her gaze flicked away, and she straightened the toiletries on the counter.

"Audrey. Talk to me. You slept with him, didn't you?"

"Um..."

"Audrey, I think you should pack up your bags and come back to Boise this instant."

Audrey frowned, unnerved with this sensible side of Ava. Usually, it was the other way around. "What? Why?"

"You just said it's not Audrey Thompson he thinks he's with. It's *me*. How do you think he'll react when he learns you're not me?"

Audrey worried her lower lip. "Maybe he doesn't need to find out."

"That'll be kind of hard to do, since he's my boss." Ava said some choice words under her breath. "Tell him the truth, then get the hell out of there. I'll figure out a way to smooth things over next time I see him."

Someone rapped on her door. "Ava? You ready?"

Anxiety and anticipation washed over her, heating her face.

"Who's that?" the real Ava blurted. She could hear when she actually listened.

Audrey called out, "Just a second," then said into the phone, "It's Zachary. We're going to his cabin." She checked her reflection one last time.

"No, you're coming home. Right?"

She couldn't meet her gaze in the mirror as she carefully turned off her phone.

****

The Jeep zipped down the highway with the top off, the wind whipping through Audrey's hair, disproving the marketing claims of Ava's super-hold hairspray. The kitchen staff had packed them a picnic basket, which they'd stored in the backseat.

Blissfully away from the Banister family

animosity, they drove into downtown Sun Valley. Zach parked on the street in front of a clothing boutique. Faceless white mannequins wearing chic summer clothes on their ultra-thin forms posed behind the storefront windows.

Audrey peered at Zach through her sunglasses. "You forget to pack something?"

"No. You did." He nodded to her short skirt and gypsy top. "Although I love looking at your legs, jeans would be more appropriate for where we're going."

Audrey looked at the fashionable mannequins again, saw dollar signs, and thought of her bank account. Crap. "I'm okay. Really." She had several pairs of jeans at home—many useless miles away.

"My treat," he said. He climbed out, then came around to open her door.

"Don't be silly. I can pay for myself." Ava, however, would have no qualms about letting him pay. She cleared her throat. "But if you insist..."

He returned her smile, and they went inside.

Zach grabbed several pairs of expensive-looking pants, plus a few shirts, all without a glance at the price tags. Audrey couldn't imagine. She shopped at Target.

He insisted she model the clothes for him. He sat in an over-stuffed chair outside the curtained dressing rooms as she changed. She'd always thought jeans were jeans, but the way these hugged her curves almost had her rethinking her frugal ways. She pushed the maroon curtain aside, feeling like Julia Roberts in *Pretty Woman*, and stepped out of the dressing room.

A huge floor-to-ceiling mirror greeted her. She turned in a slow circle in front of it and Zach. "You like?"

He hauled her onto his lap. "Hell, yes, I like," he muttered, shoving his fingers into her hair and pulling her face down to his. His mouth clamped onto hers in a hot, hard kiss. And despite the other patrons present in the store who pretended not to watch, Audrey kissed him back.

Finally, he said against her mouth, "We'd better stop before we get arrested." His hands slid down to her waist, finding bare skin as he kissed her hard again.

A few minutes later, as she rifled through a stack of T-shirts, his hand grazed the side of her breast. When he bent to pick up a pair of shoes for her, she couldn't resist running her hand across his tight behind.

By the time they finally reached the cash register, Audrey wore new blue jeans, a designer T-shirt that showed a sliver of her bare belly, and white Keds. When the saleswoman rang up the purchases, Audrey forced herself to remain upright. Holy crap! The total equaled more than her entire year's clothing budget.

When they stepped outside into the warm Sun Valley sunshine, Audrey smiled up at him. "Thank you, Zachary."

She saw her reflection in his dark shades. His eyebrows rose. "You're very welcome." He bent and kissed her nose. "Consider it a thank-you for helping me out this weekend."

"I can't imagine how generous you must be with your real girlfriends," she said, hating the thought of other women in his life.

"I like to be generous with my money." He appeared to be looking over her head and not at her. She wished she could see his eyes behind his glasses.

"You're generous with a lot of things," she said, thinking how he emphasized her sexual gratification over his own.

He said nothing, but headed toward the Jeep.

Why the reluctance to talk about this with her? She jogged to catch up with him. "Not all women expect that much generosity."

"Name one." He stopped in front of the Jeep, and tossed the bags into the back seat.

Me! Audrey wanted to shout. "Well, er, my sister. She couldn't care less about money."

"Really?" He opened the door for her. "What *does* she care about?"

Audrey climbed into her seat. Realizing she risked crossing that proverbial line, she placed a hand on his chest. The strong *ker-thunk* of his heart beat beneath her palm. "She wants a man to be generous with this."

He gave a hollow-sounding laugh, and peeled her hand from him. "That's exactly why I don't date women like your sister." When he slammed the door, Audrey jumped in her seat.

Neither spoke as they drove through Sun Valley and Ketchum, then down the highway toward Hailey, another mountain community. She needed to stop pouting; he hadn't intended to insult her. She'd invited his comment by bringing up her Audrey-self. How was he to know he'd just insulted *her*?

"How far away is your cabin?" she asked, the wind tossing her hair and her words.

The return of his grin pleased her. "It won't take long."

She leaned back in her seat and marveled at the spectacular scenery of majestic mountain peaks, bright blue sky, and gorgeous hunk of a man beside her. She needed to stop worrying about the future and savor the moment, to enjoy her life right now.

That worked until Zach pulled the Jeep into the airport.

"Where are we going?" she asked, trying to keep the panic out of her voice.

"My cabin's not accessible by car."

"Not accessible by car? Where's it at? The North Pole?"

He nudged her shoulder playfully. "Just up in the mountains a bit."

"We're already up in the mountains a bit."

"It's up a bit more."

Audrey gripped the sides of her seat as he pulled to a stop in the small parking lot. "I really think we should just stay here. I'm sure there's a nice park nearby." She rubbed her sweaty palms on the thighs of her new jeans.

He chuckled and leapt out of the vehicle, swinging the picnic basket from the backseat. "I'm sure there is, but I haven't been to my cabin in a while. I need to check on a few things."

Crap. Crap! *Crap!* Leaden legs carried her alongside Zach as they walked through the small concourse. He filed their flight plan with the flight service station, then led her outside, past a line of jets, to a small, white helicopter.

Audrey swallowed hard. "No way."

"It isn't fancy, I know, but it's fully functional."

Fully functional? Oh, that was reassuring. When he walked beneath the main rotor and reached for the door, she grabbed his arm. "Zachary. No. I can't go in that."

He turned to peer down at her, his eyes narrowing. "What are you talking about?"

"I'm...terrified of flying."

He burst out laughing. "A flight attendant afraid to fly. I've been on planes with you, Ava."

Oh, crap. She'd forgotten. But she absolutely, positively was not going up on that teensy, tiny little helicopter that was hardly bigger than her Toyota.

She grabbed his arm again. "Zach. I'm serious. I...I don't mind big planes—" Liar, liar, pants on fire. She hated *all* planes. "But a helicopter..." Panic lodged somewhere between her stomach and her throat. "Didn't you see *Black Hawk Down?*"

His brows drew together. "Those choppers were shot down in a hostile foreign country, Ava. This is Idaho."

"But..." She hugged herself, and took a step

backward.

Zach pushed his sunglasses to the top of his head, then gripped her shoulders. "You really are scared, aren't you?" he asked, studying her face.

She nodded, and looked past him to the scary machine.

He rubbed her arms. "I'm an excellent pilot, Ava. I have an unblemished safety record."

"Zach. I don't know." Yes, she *did* know. No way.

"Come on. Try it for me. It's just a short flight. I promise."

When she met his gorgeous blue eyes, she knew she was a goner. She knew another thing, too. There were now two people in this world she couldn't say no to.

****

Zach stole glances at her throughout the liftoff and ascent. Her skin had paled whiter than the surrounding snow-tipped mountains. She clenched the sides of the seat so tightly her knuckles appeared ready to break through the skin.

She looked adorable in headset and helmet. "You're doing great," he said into his mic. "We're halfway there already."

"Really?" she muttered from between clenched teeth.

"Almost."

As the chopper rose above the mountains, he said, "See, this isn't so bad, is it?"

"I'm going to be sick."

He chuckled and adjusted the cyclic pitch of the chopper, scanning the gauges in front of him. "You'll be fine."

"No, I won't."

"Talk to me. Get your mind off the flight."

"Talking won't help."

"Sure it will. Tell me about your family. You said you have a sister."

She nodded. "Audrey."

"Younger or older?"

"Same. She's my twin."

He stared at her. "Really?"

"We don't see each other much."

"You don't get along?"

"We get along great. We just have completely different lifestyles. She wouldn't know a designer label if it bit her in the butt."

Zach liked her twin already. "Is she as gorgeous as you?"

Ava didn't even smirk. "No. She's actually quite plain." In typical Ava fashion, she didn't seem to realize how conceited that sounded.

"What does she do for a living?" He kept her talking to prevent her use of the barf bag clenched in her hands.

"She teaches junior high. Lives in Boise, in a little house that actually has a picket fence. How boring is that?"

Didn't sound so bad to him.

"She's dated school principals and accountants and cable TV installers. She'll probably end up marrying someone like that and raising his kids, because she's always settled for less than her dreams." Her voice trailed off, and she closed her eyes.

"I take it a devoted husband and kids aren't your dream, Ava?"

The paper bag crunched in her fists, and she shifted in her seat. "No way. Ava Divine needs excitement in her life. Constant change, new locations, new people. Lots of money. Audrey's not into that. I guess you'd say she's pretty boring, compared to us." Her chest rose and fell with her sigh.

"I guess," he agreed, but not so sure he really did.

"I have a picture of her. Want to see it?" She looked at him, and in her eyes he saw the unmistakable gleam of uncertainty.

He nodded slowly. "Sure."

She retrieved her purse, and pulled a small picture from her wallet. "Here," she said, holding it out for him to see. "That's Audrey."

Zach stared at the photo. A sweeter, more conservative version of Ava Divine peered out at him. Unlike Ava's perfectly highlighted and styled hair, Audrey's flowed in soft, light brown waves around her shoulders. She wore hardly any makeup, and didn't have to, with her natural beauty.

He sighed. Ava seemed to be waiting for a response. "You're right. She doesn't hold a candle to you, dollface. In fact, you two don't look at all alike."

Ava slipped the photo back into her wallet. Her lips pressed tightly together. If he didn't know better, he'd think she looked hurt. "I'm going to close my eyes for a few minutes, and imagine I'm anywhere but up here," she said, her voice clipped.

He didn't mind her tuning him out, because now he could stare at her without restriction. He studied her profile, and wondered what she'd look like without makeup. Would she have that same natural beauty as her sister? That same inner glow?

He imagined combining Ava's spunk and zest for life with her sister's old-fashioned dreams, and couldn't help smiling at the thought. Did such a woman even exist?

CHAPTER 8

As far as landings went, Audrey supposed this one was good because she didn't die. She planned to kiss the ground as soon as Zach helped her from the helicopter. Then she laid eyes on the scenery she'd been too scared to look at as they descended.

Her anxiety fled, and she stood breathless.

They'd landed in a meadow, smack dab in the middle of nowhere. Heavy silence hung in the air. A breeze blew through the surrounding trees, and a blanket of violets and buttercups covered the valley floor. As she watched, an eagle soared overhead, probably hunting prey. Serenity swept through her, and she exhaled with her whole body.

Zach's remarks about her "sister" were in the past. She inhaled the floral and grassy scents. "This is beautiful. Where are we?"

"Welcome to my home," he said, grinning like a kid with a bag full of Halloween candy.

She didn't see a house, just a small, weathered outbuilding. "Where?"

He spread his hands. "All of it. Isn't it great?"

She had to agree, she thought as she bent and picked a few violets. "My favorite color," she said, lifting them to her nose.

Zach took a blossom from her fingers, and tucked it behind her ear. "There. Now you fit right in with the scenery." He grinned and reached for their bags. "Come on."

Following, she said, "Hey, I can carry my own things. You shouldn't have to do all the work."

His pace faltered a moment, then he resumed his stride toward the outbuilding. Opening a wide door, he gestured to a four-wheeler. "You ever ride on one of these?"

She stepped across the planked floor, glad Zach had bought her some tennis shoes. "Not since I was a kid."

He attached their things to the back of the ATV, then climbed on, motioning her up behind him.

She swung her leg over the seat, then gripped his shoulders as she adjusted her position. The machine coughed to life, and pulled out onto the lush grass.

The vehicle vibrated over the bumpy ground. Audrey slipped her hands around Zach's waist. His rock-hard abs tensed at her touch.

"Where are we going?" she called over the roar of the engine, pressing her inner thighs against his hips to keep from falling off.

"Somewhere really beautiful."

"More beautiful than this?"

"Trust me," he said.

They entered the forest. Sunlight filtered through the tall Austrian pines, and the shade cooled her skin. Twice, they startled a deer in their path, not to mention countless rabbits.

A few minutes later, the trees disappeared and they entered a clearing. Audrey swore she'd never doubt Zach's word again. A rustic log cabin nestled on the opposite side of the field, framed by cottonwood and firs.

When he cut the engine and the silence of Mother Nature enveloped them, she heard the wind blowing through the forest and whistling in the tall grasses.

"This *is* gorgeous," she whispered, hating to break the solitude. "It's like something out of a storybook. Can we go inside?"

"Sure."

She glanced at him sideways and smirked. "Last one there's a rotten egg!" She sprinted ahead, but his footsteps pounded on the grass behind her.

As she neared the cabin, Zach's arm snaked around her waist and he hauled her out of his way. He slapped the log siding in triumph.

Breathing hard, Audrey planted her hands on her hips. "No fair. You cheated."

"Yeah, so?"

She swatted his arm, then stepped past him. She wiggled the doorknob, expecting it to be locked, but the door creaked open. "Didn't your mama warn you to lock your doors?"

Zach entered the cabin first. "My mama was more concerned with making sure we knew which fork to use," he said. "I keep this unlocked for backpackers. Gives them a place to shelter."

"That's thoughtful," she gushed, really looking at this man, and seeing someone she'd never expected.

He shrugged off the compliment. "Have a look around while I check on a couple of things. Then we'll eat."

The cabin consisted of a single room. The only lighting came from the four windows, one on each wall. A wood stove with a couple of burners stood in the corner, a gigantic rack of antlers hanging above it. Probably a distant relative of her favorite deer head.

"I don't even want to know what happened to your head," she muttered to the antlers.

"What?" Zach paused in the doorway.

"Just talking to Bambi." She motioned over her shoulder.

He grinned and disappeared outside.

Open wooden shelves lined one wall of the kitchen area, filled with canned food, books, and outdoor necessities. A sturdy wooden table with two chairs occupied another corner, and pushed in front of the fireplace was a double bed piled high with folded quilts, blankets, and pillows.

"How often do you come here?" she asked when he returned, charmed by the whole thing.

"As often as I can," he said, "which isn't nearly often enough."

"Alone?" she ventured.

He shot her a raised-eyebrow look. "Usually."

"I bet this goes over really well with the ladies."

He laughed, but didn't sound amused. "The fact that you entered the cabin without making little sounds of disgust under your breath puts you in a league of your own."

"Are you serious? What kind of women have you brought up here?"

"Your kind, actually."

Unexpected hurt welled up inside her, then she realized he referred to Ava's kind.

He turned toward the open door. "Come on. You haven't seen the best part."

She pulled her sunglasses onto her nose and stepped into the sunlight. Zach disappeared around the corner of the cabin.

As she circled the structure, she stopped in her tracks. "Oh, my," she said.

A clear mountain stream gurgled twenty feet from the cabin, lined with boulders big enough to lie on.

"Beautiful, isn't it?"

She nodded, moving toward the water. She bent and wriggled her fingers in it. "Ooh. It's freezing."

"We're in the mountains, Ava."

Ava. How she'd love to hear him call her "Audrey," to know he'd brought Audrey to his special place. She straightened and wiped her wet hands onto her jeans, forcing a neutral expression onto her face. "So, is this some sort of test you give the women in your life?" Not that *she* was in his life.

One of his brows lifted. "Am I that obvious?"

She watched the water skim over the smooth stones. "Um, what happens if they fail?" Her belly tightened.

"Then we leave."

"And you never see them again."

He shrugged. "I wouldn't go that far, but..."

"And if they pass?" She suspended her breath as she awaited his answer.

"I've yet to see that happen."

"You don't trust easily, do you?" She kept her voice calm. "The test list must be long."

"Three. Including you."

"Incl—" She blinked, realizing the magnitude of his words. When she found her voice, she said, "How could any woman in her right mind not love it?" She sat on a flat rock and looked around, at the back of the darling cabin, at the trees, at the tips of the rugged mountain peaks, at the stream and colorful flora and fauna surrounding it. "This is heaven."

When he didn't respond, she turned to find him staring at her. His blue eyes held hers, an unspoken question in their depths.

Butterflies flitted through her stomach like the ones on the nearby wildflowers. If she thought for a moment it was Audrey Thompson who was "passing" his little test, she'd be elated. Even as Ava, though, her heart rate picked up.

She turned her gaze to the rippling water, letting its soothing gurgles wash over her frazzled nerve endings.

Zach climbed onto her boulder, then leapt over the narrow stream and planted himself on another big rock. Part of her wished he'd stayed beside her, close enough to touch, but the sensible part of her was glad he'd given her some breathing room.

"You're right about me," he finally said, his eyes focused on the water.

"In what way?"

"About me not trusting women. When you grow up in a wealthy family, you get used to people wanting you for your money." He hurled a small rock into the water. The splash disappeared into the slow-moving current. "Everyone has an ulterior motive. Most people aren't upfront about who they are and what they want."

Audrey looked away, her face hot with guilt. She stared up at the blue sky, watching the breeze carry the clouds over the trees and out of her sight. The creek gurgled and bubbled beneath her. "What was her name?"

"Who?"

"The woman who broke your heart. The woman you last brought up here with such high hopes."

He sat with his legs bent, his forearms propped on his knees. "Rachel," he said, his voice quiet.

"Tell me."

He shrugged. "There's not much to tell. We dated. It got serious. Then I found out she wasn't who she said she was."

Thud. Audrey's heart took a nosedive, and landed in the pit of her stomach. "What happened?" Thankfully, her voice didn't give away her guilty conscience.

"It was a match set up by our parents. It would be good for business, merging the two family companies. Rachel was in on it the whole time."

"That doesn't mean she didn't love you."

He sneered. "She loved my money. All her talk about wanting to settle down and raise a family was just a con."

Audrey stared at him, surprised. Ava had told her he was a confirmed bachelor who balked at commitments. She let this information sink in. Hope tap-danced around her heart.

"Anyway," he said, "I'm more careful now about who I trust." His tone conveyed his desire to end the Rachel talk.

His words presented the perfect segue for her to come clean, to let him know he could trust her, but the timing didn't feel right. Not yet, anyway. "I know what you mean about feeling used," she said, her voice quiet. "Growing up, everyone compared me to my sister. Ava was always the beautiful one, the popular one, the one all the boys flocked to."

"That must have been really hard on Audrey." He looked relieved to have changed the subject.

Audrey met his gaze. Oh. Crap. She'd almost blown it. "She hated it," she admitted, needing to be truthful in some capacity with him. "Every time a boy asked her out, she would wonder in the back of her mind if he was using her to get to Ava—er, me."

Zach stretched out on his rock, belly down, facing her with his chin resting on his folded arms. "I would imagine you face that to some extent, too."

She lay down in similar fashion. "In what way?"

"Do you ever wonder if a man is interested in you for yourself, or is it just your beauty and amazing body?"

She'd never really considered that. Did Ava have that problem, and did her sister even care?

Then Zach's words hit her on another level. Did he really think *she* was beautiful with an amazing body, or was he talking about Ava?

"I-I guess I've never cared one way or another." She blushed and dropped her gaze.

"I'll be honest with you, dollface. Before this weekend, I never really made it past your looks. I know that sounds shallow of me, but I'm a man. Comes with the territory."

"Thanks for the tip," she murmured, feeling the tug on her lips. "I think it's hard to make it past a person's exterior, and see what's inside. Even when you think you know them, you don't."

"Are you referring to yourself, or to me?"

She rolled to her back, and shielded her eyes with the crook of her arm. "Mostly myself, I suppose. What you see or think you see isn't always what you get, and what you get isn't always what you want."

At the slap of Zach's shoes on her rock, she

scooted over to make room for him, and he stretched out beside her.

"Why don't you let me be the judge of what I want and don't want," he said softly. He lifted a hand and trailed the backs of his fingers across her cheek and jaw line.

She closed her eyes, wanting to believe what he said and did was really meant for Audrey Thompson's benefit. It would be so easy to believe...she *wanted* to believe.

His fingers moved to her lips, lingering over her lower one. "Kiss me, Ava."

"Zach," she whispered, opening her eyes, sensing they had headed into uncharted emotional territory.

He misread the hesitation in her eyes. "Don't worry," he said. "God knows I'm in no hurry to jump into anything serious. But..." He looked up to the sky, the filtered sun through the trees mottling his face. "I like what's going on here. I think it's worth pursuing." He trailed his hand down the side of her neck.

Something worth pursuing, she repeated silently. He leaned toward her, his warm breath fractions away from her mouth. His lips touched hers.

The tender and searching kiss inspired Audrey to explore this new territory with him...but as Audrey. Not as Ava.

"Zach." Her stomach muscles tightened as he swirled a lazy finger around her belly button. "I'm not who you think I am."

"I like who you are, dollface." He pushed her shirt up, and released the clasp of her bra. Moving the pink lace cups and gel falsies aside, he said, "You won't be needing these up here." The cool mountain breeze brushed across her bare breasts, teasing her exposed nipples into hard peaks. His lips closed over one, sucking it fully into his hot mouth.

She arched off the warm rock. "I'm serious. You

need to—" She suspended her breath when his hand slipped into her pants.

"I know exactly what I need." He nibbled at her breast as his fingers played with her sex. Her hips writhed beneath his touch. After a few minutes of heaven, he rose over her and unbuttoned her jeans, pulling them off along with her shoes, then tossing them onto the bank. He cupped her knees and spread her legs, then lowered his face between her thighs. She closed her eyes as he kissed the dark triangle of pubic hair.

His tongue found her center. Her buttocks tightened on the hard rock beneath her. She should make him stop. He pushed two fingers into her hot sheath. She was already wet, and her slickness wrapped around his digits.

She'd never stop him now, nor did she want to. She wanted him, any way she could get him. She would figure out later how to prove to him that he could trust her. She speared her fingers into his hair and pulled him closer.

"I want you inside me," she gasped out as his fingers drove her relentlessly toward climax.

"I'm not done tasting you yet," he said, his words vibrating against her. Her hips bucked in response.

"Zach, please." She needed that connection, and she needed it now.

"If you insist." He kissed her sensitive nub, then withdrew from her. He sat on his heels and reached into his back pocket, pulling out his wallet. He extracted a condom, and held it between his teeth as he slipped off his shoes and jeans. He quickly sheathed himself, then lay back on the rock in all his naked glory. "Come on up here, baby. Climb aboard."

She straddled his hips, watching his eyes. Reaching between them, she positioned his straining penis at her opening. His lids grew heavy, his irises darkening to midnight as she lowered herself onto him.

"Holy hell, you're hot...and tight," he said between gritted teeth. He reached for the hem of her shirt and pulled it over her head.

As she shrugged out of the unclasped bra, she said, "You're sure we're alone up here?"

"Except for the occasional wild animal, yeah." He fondled her breasts as she rode him. "God, I love being inside you."

And I love you, she thought, angling her face to the sky, eyes closed, enjoying the sensation.

Wait. She loved him?

Sure, he made her feel things she'd never felt before, sexually and otherwise, but love?

He caressed her swollen clit, the juices from their lovemaking allowing his finger to glide easily. "You keep doing that, mister, and this'll be over before we've barely begun." She braced her hands on his thighs behind her hips, arching her breasts toward the sky.

"That's what I want, baby," he said, changing the angle of his caress. "I want you to come for me." He pinched her nipple hard between his thumb and forefinger.

"Mm, yes," she cried. Pressure welled inside her, warming and tickling her limbs from the inside all the way down to her toes. Her bare knees dug into the hard rock beneath his body. "I'm going to—"

She exploded in orgasm. As she tightened and pulsed around him, he cried out his own release, digging his fingers into her hips.

She collapsed on top of him, and his arms wrapped around her. "My knees are all scraped up," she said, breathless.

"Yeah, well, at least your ass and back aren't rubbed raw," he said, kissing her neck.

She giggled against his chest. "This was your idea."

"I'd do it again for you, baby. But let's get off this rock first."

CHAPTER 9

Zach enjoyed the next few hours more than any he could recall in recent memory. After catching four trout in the stream, he and Ava gutted the fish and cooked them over an open grill. To his surprise and shock, she'd helped clean the fish, *and* didn't seem too grossed out by it.

Ava confused him. On one hand, she was the Ava Divine of old, with her perfectly manicured nails and flawless makeup and hair. On the other hand, she was down-to-earth, laid back, and genuine. And hot damn, both sides of her personality turned him on.

He glanced across the barbecue pit to where she collected a bouquet of wildflowers from the surrounding meadow. Warmth gathered in his stomach just looking at her, and not all of it lust. When had he last felt so comfortable around a woman, so able to be himself, flaws and all?

A cool raindrop splashed on his lap, and then another. The temperature dropped noticeably. He checked his watch. "Hey, dollface. We'd better get going soon. We don't have a lot of light left."

She looked up from her bent-over position, the neck of her T-shirt gaping just enough for him to see down her shirt. She'd delighted him by ditching the bra and falsies when she dressed after their romp on the rocks. Her rosy nipples hung like bells on her gently swaying breasts. He stuffed his suddenly itchy hands into his jeans pockets.

"So soon? I'm not ready to go yet," she said.

He grinned, and his heart swelled. Whenever he was here, he didn't want to leave either, never knowing when he'd get back again.

The rain fell faster. She shielded her eyes and looked at the gray clouds overhead. "What about the rain?"

He shrugged. "A little rain never hurt anyone."

"No, I mean what about the rain and flying? I don't want to fly in a storm."

He looked up. Heavy gray clouds had darkened the sky. "If we leave now, we should beat the worst of it."

"The worst of it? I don't want to fly in the best of it, Zachary." She wrapped her arms around her body. "If this is anything like Boise, it will blow through real quick. We could wait."

"That'll mean flying in the dark, which is okay with me, but..." He met her worried gaze.

The distant sound of thunder ripped over the mountain peaks. She gnawed her lower lip. "Can't we just stay here until morning?"

"There's no running water, no electricity. None of the amenities you're used to." Not to mention just one bed. The thought of holding her in his arms all night thrilled him and freaked him out at the same time. The more time he spent with her, the more he liked her. The more he liked her, the tighter his heart squeezed in his chest. He didn't know if he should run with that feeling, or run away.

She looked to the sky again. "I really don't want to fly in this. Flying in nice weather was bad enough." Her brows furrowed, and her lips thinned. "I'm sorry, Zach. I know I'm being a wuss about this. But—"

He held up his hand. "No apology necessary. We'll stay. I wasn't ready to leave yet either."

Her smile lit up the darkening skies. "Thank you."

He shrugged off her thanks, not minding in the slightest that he was going to be holed up in a tiny cabin in the middle of nowhere with a woman whose beauty rivaled their surroundings.

He would just ignore the little voice in his head telling him to run for the hills.

****

A chill settled over the pristine valley, and Audrey wished she'd brought something warmer to wear.

She stood beside the cabin and watched Zach gather a stack of firewood. Rubbing her arms and feeling goose bumps, she asked, "Won't your family be worried when we don't show up?"

"I radioed the airport and told them of our situation. If the family gets worried, they'll call the tower. Besides, it's not like I can't take care of myself."

"Can I help?" She motioned to the firewood.

He shook his head. "You'll scratch your arms."

"So will you."

He met her gaze. "Ava Divine wants to carry firewood." One corner of his mouth turned upward, as if he couldn't decide whether to smile or frown. Guilt nagged Audrey's conscience. He shook his head. "Thanks, though," he said.

"In all the time you've known me," she asked, knowing she had to tread cautiously, "have I really come across as so helpless?"

He straightened with his load of firewood. "In some ways."

"Are most of the women you date helpless?"

"In the ways I think we're talking about, yes."

"Do you find that attractive in a woman?"

She held the door for him, and he paused to shoot her a long look. "I find *you* attractive, dollface." He kissed her on the mouth before brushing past her into the tiny cabin. "I think everyone should do what they're capable of, and not always rely on others to do it for them."

"Well then, I can certainly carry firewood. I've even been known to start a fire or two in my fireplace at home."

He dumped the logs next to the wood stove, then began stacking them. "Two days ago, that would have shocked the hell out of me. But now—" He grinned at her.

She grinned back. "You know, it sounds to me like you need to find a new place to meet women. Most of my girlfriends can carry firewood, too. Then there is, um, my sister, who insists on heating her entire house with her wood stove each winter rather than turning on the heat, because she thinks it's cozy and romantic." She forced herself to breathe normally, as if she didn't care one way or another how he reacted to a glimpse of her true self.

"Imagine that," he said without looking at her.

"She actually went into the hills with a friend to cut her own firewood last fall."

Zach brushed his hands off on his jeans, then squatted in front of the fireplace and began piling twigs and kindling. "Your sister sounds like quite the trooper."

Not quite the romantic description Audrey would have liked. "She is. She'd love this place, too. She's a nature girl."

He didn't respond as he stacked logs atop the kindling, and lit the stack with a long matchstick.

Audrey watched him a moment longer before grabbing their empty water container and heading outside. As she knelt beside the stream and scooped up some clear water, she couldn't help thinking that her Audrey-self and Zach seemed to have a lot in common. Maybe she was *too* self-sufficient for him. He might *say* he wanted a woman who could do things for herself, but when it came right down to it...

She wondered if Zach really even knew what he was looking for. He'd been handed his life on a silver platter. He had more than enough money to buy whatever he wanted, yet something seemed to be missing from his life.

She'd have liked to think it was her.

Giving herself a mental shake, she headed back into the cabin. Zach stood before a blazing fire, hands on hips, the amber light casting the front of his body in bronze and gold. He glanced at the water container in her hands. "What's that for?"

"I saw some packets of hot cocoa on the shelf. Doesn't a warm drink sound yummy?"

He grinned, the firelight dancing off his jet-black hair. "As a matter of fact, it does." His gaze raked her body, stopping at her chest.

She didn't need to look down to know her nipples strained against the white cotton shirt. They were still tender from their lovemaking beside the creek. The soft material had been chafing against the sensitive peaks for the past couple of hours. "I'll, uh, see to the cocoa."

She busied herself with the thoughtless tasks of cleaning the teakettle and mugs, and hunting down a spoon.

A few minutes later, the kettle whistled. She poured the hot water into the waiting mugs and stirred in the cocoa powder, the sweet chocolate scent mingling with the smell of woodsmoke. With mugs in each hand and a couple of granola bars under one arm, she headed to the fireplace, where Zach had scooted the chairs from the table.

"Here you go," she said, handing him the drink and snack.

She shivered as she sat down and took a sip of hot chocolate. The fire popped and crackled in front of her. "Mmm. I was getting cold." She stretched her feet toward the warm flames.

Zach set his cup on the table and stood. He returned with a quilt from the bed. "Here," he said, wrapping it around her shoulders. "I'm sorry I didn't think of this earlier. You're probably freezing."

As he sat next to her, she said, "I have two

working feet. I could have gotten it myself."

He sipped his drink, the steam rising above the mug and shielding his face. "*Touché*, Miss Divine," he said, lifting the mug in a mock salute.

As the sun finished setting behind the mountains around the cabin, the last vestiges of light faded from the small room, save the flickering firelight.

Audrey stifled a yawn with the back of her wrist. "What time is it?"

He tilted his watch toward the fire. "A little past ten."

Together, they put clean sheets on the bed and covered it with the thick quilts. Zach had some clothes hidden in the cabin, so he lent her one of his T-shirts for sleeping. When he went outside to visit Mother Nature's little boys' room, she quickly shed her clothes, slipped his shirt over her head, then jumped into the bed. She'd no sooner pulled the quilt up to her chin when he reentered the cabin.

He added more wood to the fire, then approached the edge of the bed. He stripped off his shirt. Even in the dim light, his body stunned her, all angles and planes, muscle and bone. Not an ounce of flab. She resisted the urge to lick her lips, turning her head away instead.

"You're either nervous, or cold," he said quietly.

"Actually," she cleared her throat, "I'm both."

Silence pervaded the cabin. Finally, he said, "Actually...I'm both, too."

She met his gaze in the dim firelight. "It's not like we haven't—like we've never..." Man, she couldn't even get out a complete sentence.

Zach sat on the edge of the mattress. "Sharing a bed is probably the most intimate act between a man and a woman. You're completely vulnerable when you're asleep. You have to really trust the person you're with."

She stared up at the dark ceiling as rain began

to batter the roof of the tiny cabin. "I want you to trust me, Zach."

"I do trust you, dollface."

"No, you don't. Not completely." She rolled onto her side and propped herself onto an elbow. "But I know how you can."

"How?"

"You have to get naked first."

A slow grin moved across his face. "I like the way you think, Miss Divine." He stripped off his jeans, revealing his growing erection.

"Now lie down in the middle of the bed." She climbed off the mattress to make room. He started to pull the quilt over his body, but she stopped him.

"Sweetheart, cold air does disastrous things to a man."

She grinned, and crossed the room to the shelves on the opposite wall. "So I've heard," she called over her shoulder. "Lucky for you, you have a lot to work with."

"Thank you for that." He chuckled.

She scanned the shelves, and found what she'd seen when she'd first come into the cabin this afternoon.

"What are you doing way over there?" he asked, his voice playful and pouty.

"Good things come to those who wait," she said. She stalked toward the bed.

When he saw the rope in her hands, he shook his head and sat up. "Sweetheart, I don't trust *anyone* that much."

"Please, Zach," she said in a soft voice as she knelt on the bed. "I really need you to trust me."

Something in her voice made him believe her, despite all the warning bells in his head. He realized he'd rather face his demons than hurt her with a refusal. When she pushed at his chest, he obeyed and lay back down.

She reached for one of his hands, holding it up

to her face and drawing each finger into her mouth one at a time, all the while not breaking his gaze. The gentle suction of her lips around his digits had him growing harder by the second. She stretched his arm over his head, and tied his wrist to the bedpost. She followed the same sexy routine with his other hand. The moment both his wrists were bound, adrenaline and something else—anxiety?—shot through his body. He tugged against the restraints, and found her knots solid.

"Ava..." His voice was strained.

She leaned over him, her long hair tickling his face as she kissed him long and deep. "Trust me," she whispered against his lips.

He hated not being able to wrap his arms around her. She left his mouth, and trailed hot kisses across his jaw and down his neck. Her tongue swirled around one of his nipples, pebbling it immediately, then she moved to the other. He gasped as her teeth bit gently into the sensitive skin.

"Ava."

"Shh," she murmured, moving lower. Her tongue dipped into his belly button, and he lifted his hips in response. She giggled. "My, you're sensitive, Mr. Banister. And I haven't even gotten to the good part yet."

The good part pointed straight in the air as she approached it. She kissed against his pubic hair. She kissed and licked around the base of his shaft, reaching between his legs and fondling his balls as she moved down to his thighs.

She reached his foot and started to wrap the rope around his ankle.

"No. Tying my arms is one thing, but—" His words cut off when she took him into her mouth. God.

She looked up at him from beneath hooded lids, her mouth full. Then her clever tongue licked a heated circle around the head. His entire body jerked. She pulled away long enough to ask, "Do you trust me, Zach?" Then she pressed her tongue into the slit at the tip, and the electric shock torpedoed his resistance.

If he could trust her with his dick in her mouth, he supposed he might as well go all the way. He nodded. She grinned, then tied his feet to the footboard, one at a time. When she was done, she leaned across him to check all the knots, her hair teasing his already over-sensitized skin. Despite the freezing air in the cabin, he burned with need and eagerness.

She maneuvered herself between his spread-eagled legs and planted her hands on either side of his hips. With another sultry glance and a smile, she dipped her head and took him all the way into her mouth. Slowly, she pulled away, grazing her teeth against his skin before taking him deep again. Her hot tongue swirled around the tip, pressing against the slit, tasting him. Killing him.

His hands clenched and unclenched as she grasped the base of his penis and stroked in time with her sucking mouth. His feet flexed and strained against the ropes, the coarse hemp digging into his skin.

"Please, Ava. Untie me. I want to hold you."

"No." She continued to suck on him, driving him just to the edge before pulling away.

"Untie me."

"No. Not until you realize you can trust me." She fondled him with her hand. "Every time we've been intimate, you've done all the work. This time, it's my turn. So my suggestion to you is quit trying to run things, relax, and enjoy the show."

With her expert mouth and hands, she coaxed him into flight. She licked a slow path from the base of his cock to the very tip, and his blood roared through his ears like a jet engine taking off down the runway. She wrapped her lips over the head, her fingers around his shaft. Her gentle but insistent pumping with her mouth and hands lifted his hips off the mattress, and he strained against his bindings. God! The pressure inside him picked up speed, and the back of his head pressed into the pillow.

He couldn't take much more of this before he—

Heat ripped through his body like a lightning bolt. His release roared into the stillness of the cabin as he spurted his hot seed deep into her throat. She continued licking and caressing until she'd extracted every last bit of pleasure from him. He shuddered and bucked at every touch of her tongue and lips around his sensitive organ.

Finally, he collapsed, sated and exhausted, his ankles and wrists limp against the restraints. She draped herself across his still heaving torso. He ached to run his hands across her hair and down her back. He tugged against the ropes. "Any chance I can talk you into untying me?"

"I'm not done with you yet." She climbed off the bed, and crossed her arms to pull the T-shirt over her head. Then she bent and slipped out of her lacy panties. Gloriously naked, her skin shone golden in the firelight.

"God, you're beautiful, Ava."

She smiled and climbed back onto the bed, straddling his hips. Placing her hands on either side of his head, she bent forward until her breasts dangled right over his face. He had to turn his head only a fraction to catch a rosy nipple in his mouth. She moaned at the contact, her hair falling across her face and onto his, tickling his sensitized skin.

As she moved on top of him, Zach felt his penis coming to life again. It poked against her hot opening. "I have condoms in my bag," he muttered, pulling against the ropes.

"I'm on the pill," she said. She wriggled her hips against him, teasing him.

"You trust me enough not to use a condom?"

"Do you trust me enough to believe I'm on the pill?"

He stared into her eyes, fringed by dark lashes, and knew he could. He would trust this woman with his life. He nodded, lifting his head off the soft pillow, willing her mouth forward. As she leaned in to kiss him, his penis slipped inside her hot, tight folds.

He groaned at the intimate contact, skin to skin. "You feel amazing," he whispered against her mouth. He gave up fighting his ropes, and let her have her way with him. She rode him hard, her breasts bobbing with her frantic movements, her hair a wild, sweaty mess. God, she turned him on. Made him hot. Drove him *crazy*. Her vagina squeezed his shaft as she rose and fell, over and over, her bare bottom slapping against his pelvis. Her nipples hardened, casting shadows across her breasts.

"Touch yourself, dollface," he urged, knowing he couldn't last much longer, wanting, *needing* them to come together.

She did, and within seconds she arched her back, screaming her orgasm into the quiet cabin. The spasming of her tight walls took him right over the edge, and he exploded into her, bucking off the mattress, his wrists and ankles jerking against their tethers.

She collapsed on top of him, breathing heavily. His heart pounded in his ribcage, and he wondered if she could feel it beneath her cheek. As if she sensed his thoughts, one of her hands splayed across his chest, right over his heart.

He knew at that moment he loved her. He trusted her, heart and soul. For the first time in his life, he'd let himself be completely vulnerable with a woman. And also for the first time, he allowed himself to dream that maybe, just maybe, he'd found someone he could grow old with.

She moved off him, and he immediately missed her warmth. Before he could ask where she was going, she'd untied one of his hands, then the other, caressing and rubbing his wrists where they'd chafed against the ropes. She moved to the end of the bed and untied his feet, treating his sore ankles to the same loving attention. Then she climbed in next to him, snuggling up against his body as he wrapped his freed arms around her. He inhaled the flowery scent of her hair, kissed the top of her head, and fell sound asleep.

CHAPTER 10

The next morning, Audrey woke to the sound of tap, tap, tapping against the log cabin wall and the feel of strong, male arms around her waist.

"Good morning," Zach whispered, pulling her tighter against him, spoon-fashion.

She turned in his arms. "Morning," she said. One long look into the deep blue of his eyes, and she realized there was no other place she'd rather be.

He moved his head enough to kiss her softly on the mouth. "I like waking up with you in my arms," he said.

She smiled. "I like it, too." She snuggled deeper into his embrace. His chest rose and fell against her back, and his warm breath whispered in her hair.

"Last night was amazing," he said.

She smiled against his forearm. "Glad you enjoyed yourself."

Silence pervaded the cabin as he held her. Finally, he said, "Do you ever wonder if things are too good to be true?" His quiet words conveyed a serious tone.

Without turning to face him, she asked, "Are you talking about right now?"

He kissed her shoulder and pulled her even closer. "I could stay like this forever, here in this cabin, in this bed, with you."

His words were like a straight shot of hard liquor—a jolt of pleasure and warmth through her veins, followed by a bittersweet aftertaste. "Are you worried that when we head back to civilization, things will be different?"

"It's pretty perfect right now."

"And you don't think perfect can last?" Her chest tightened as she waited for his answer.

He didn't say anything for a long time. Finally, he said, "I don't know. I've never had perfect before."

Audrey's eyes burned with tears. "Me, either," she said, her voice raw. "Whenever I thought I did...Well, um, *Audrey* says it's kind of like that scene in *The Wizard of Oz* where Dorothy's all excited and ready to go home. Everything is great...and then the balloon leaves without her."

"I've been left behind by that proverbial balloon a few times in my life." His warm breath ruffled the hair at her temple. "Do you think this balloon is going to take off without you?"

She refused to think about it, and curled her fingers around his arm. "I hope not," she said honestly. That brought another warm kiss to her shoulder. "You know, another thing that Audrey says is—"

Zach pressed her into the pillows, and stared down at her. "Dollface. That's the second time in the past minute you've brought up your sister."

Audrey looked away, her cheeks buzzing with warmth.

He guided her chin with his index finger until their gazes locked. "I'm thinking that maybe you're a little envious of her. I think you're jealous of Audrey."

"You don't understand."

"I think I do. From what you've told me, your sister is happy. Even though her life might be humble, she has everything she needs. While you and me..." He glanced away a moment. "We're cut from the same cloth. We've spent a lot of time pretending to know what we've needed, but actually having no clue. Everything we need has been right in front of our noses for a while now. We just didn't bother sitting still long enough to see it."

She had to ask. "Do you want what Audrey has?

Would you be happy with her life?"

Zach gave her a gentle smile, almost as if he felt sorry for her, then turned her until she was cradled against him. "I'm sure your sister is a lovely person, but I don't want what she has. I want what *I* have right now." He kissed the top of her head.

Audrey batted back tears. She'd dug herself a hole, and would have a heck of a time climbing back out. On a long breath, she relaxed into his arms. She didn't want to think about that now. Like Zach said, she wanted what she had right now, too.

They stayed like that until the sun came up over the mountains and spilled its light through the tiny, dust-covered windows of the cabin. Audrey knew they'd have to get up eventually, but she'd let him make the first move.

She heard the tap, tap, tapping again. "What's that?"

"Woodpecker. I'd have thrown something at the wall to scare it, but I didn't want to wake you."

He was so sweet. So different than the man she'd first assumed. "Mmm," she murmured, cozying back into his arms. His erection pressed against her hip. "Speaking of peckers," she said.

He choked on a laugh, and flipped her onto her back. "That's what I love about you, dollface. I never know what you're going to say or do."

Love.

She stared up into his handsome face, and realized exactly what she loved about him.

Him.

As soon as they returned to Sun Valley, she'd tell him the truth, despite her fears and anxiety. Telling him here, right now, wouldn't give him the space he might need to let the information sink in. She pulled his face down and captured his mouth with hers, scraping her fingernails down his back until he was as caught up in the moment as she.

He spread her thighs with his knees. Poising at

the brink of her femininity, he leaned down to kiss her mouth at the same time he entered her.

"Oh, dollface," he groaned into her ear as they neared climax. "I adore you."

The dam around her heart burst, flooding her soul with pleasure and pain. *Please, please, please let him adore the real me. Please let him understand why I lied to him.*

He might be thinking he was loving Ava Divine, but it was Audrey Thompson who loved him back.

****

Zach kept a close eye on Audrey throughout the short flight back to the Sun Valley Airport. He told himself his concern was over her fear of flying, which he still thought rather ironic. But he knew in his heart the real reason: he'd fallen for her. Hard.

As they approached the airport, her lips pressed tightly together, and she looked about as rigid as the blades on the rotor. "You doing okay?"

She nodded without looking his way. She'd told him earlier if she moved her head, she might throw up.

The primal need to protect her tugged at his heartstrings. "We're almost there. Just a few more minutes."

"If I never see a helicopter again, it'll be too soon."

"That's too bad, because the only other way to reach my cabin is to hike in."

She looked this time. "You're inviting me back?"

He grinned. "Absolutely."

A flush lit her face, and she smiled. "Okay. Maybe I can manage this flight again. But next time, I'm bringing tequila."

Once they were on the ground and back in his Jeep, she checked her reflection in the tiny mirror on the visor and gave a loud sigh. "Well, here goes the game again." She rummaged through her purse, and pulled out a tube of lipstick.

He worked his jaw a few moments. "It's not a game for me anymore, dollface."

He felt her gaze on him. He stared at the road ahead, shocked at what he was about to say to her. "I'm in love with you." He had to shout it over the wind rushing through the topless vehicle.

She didn't say anything, the lipstick poised over her lips. She bowed her head and closed the lipstick tube, lowering her hands to her lap.

Zach's heart spiraled to the ground, a nosedive to the gut. He should have known better than to blurt out his feelings like that. She'd told him time and time again how she didn't want to get serious with anyone, how her career and life were fine without a man.

He floored the Jeep, and they drove the rest of the way back to his family's estate in silence.

As he pulled up to the eight-car garage behind the house, he said quietly, "I've scared you off."

For a moment, he worried she wouldn't respond. "You scared me," she admitted, and his stomach plunged a thousand feet. "But you didn't scare me off."

He swiveled in his seat. "You haven't said a word for the past ten minutes."

She finally met his gaze, and he saw moisture rimming her beautiful green eyes, making them sparkle like the stream behind his cabin. "I've never felt like this before, Zachary. Ever. And I've never felt the urge to tell a man other than my father that I loved him, but..." A tear spilled onto her cheek. "We barely know each other. You...don't really know me." Her throat contracted with a hard swallow.

He sucked in a long breath. "I've been with enough women to know when something is different, special. I've never felt this way, either. I don't think it matters if we've known each other a day, a year, or a decade."

He pulled her into his arms, and she opened to

him without hesitation.

A few minutes later, as they walked up the cobblestone path to the house, she said, "There's something I need to tell you before we take our relationship any farther."

But before she could utter another word, the double doors swung open in front of them, and his mother stepped out. "Well, it's about time you returned. You'll never guess who's here."

Warning bells went off in Zach's head. His mother only looked that pleased with herself when she had something up her sleeve. He held back a groan, and waited for the bomb to drop.

His mother, seeing she had their full attention, said, "It's Ava's twin sister. Audrey."

****

Audrey's feet ground to a stop, embedded in concrete. Ava? In Sun Valley? Oh, God.

"Are you all right?" Zach asked, turning to look at her.

No, she wasn't all right. She was going to throw up. All over her designer jeans. "I-I'm fine," she managed to sputter. More like shell-shocked.

Moving like a robot, she stepped inside the foyer and came face-to-face with Ava—dressed as Audrey, wearing beige capris, pink tank top, and slip-on flats.

"Surprise," Ava-as-Audrey greeted them, coming forward to wrap Audrey into a hug.

"What are you doing here?" Audrey whispered into her twin's ear.

"Saving you," Ava hissed back. She pulled away, and Audrey thought her legs might buckle beneath her. The real Ava turned to Zach. "You must be Zachary Banister." She held out her hand and waited for him to shake it. "I've heard a lot about you. Gosh, I feel like I already know you."

Audrey wanted to strangle her. She watched Zach's face carefully, waiting to see when he figured it out. But he just smiled and shook Ava's hand.

"It's nice to meet you, Audrey," he said. "I've heard a lot of nice things about you, too."

Ava pressed her hand to her heart. "Well, you know what they say about twins—we're always on each other's minds."

Audrey wanted to punch her. She wanted to scream, to cry, to do something to get out of this mess, but she was paralyzed.

"I'm just making sure my sister isn't getting herself into too much trouble. You know how she can be."

Zach smiled, and gave Audrey's waist a squeeze. "Don't worry. I've kept a good eye on her." She knew he probably expected her to look up at him, but she couldn't.

Finally, she choked, "When did you get here, *Audrey*?" She practically spat out her own name.

"I just flew in. I was about to share some tea with Mrs. Banister. She's been a perfectly lovely hostess."

Audrey grabbed her sister's arm, pleased to hear the soft gasp of pain. "Tea does sound perfectly lovely." Gag. "But I really need to get cleaned up first. *Audrey*, you can keep me company." With a frazzled smile in Zach's direction, and a quick glance toward Mrs. Banister's smug expression, Audrey dragged her sister across the marble foyer and up the curving staircase.

She didn't stop until they were inside her room with the door safely closed behind them. She swung around to face Ava. "What the heck are you doing here?" Her skin burned, and her stomach felt like she'd just done a thousand sit-ups.

"'Hell,' Aud. You can say 'hell.' It's a bit more apropos than 'heck' when you're this uptight." Dropping all pretenses, Ava sashayed across the floor, then plopped onto the edge of the bed. "Like I told you, I'm here to save you."

"Save me from what?"

Ava studied her short fingernails as if they held the secret to world peace. "I can't believe I removed my nails for you. Oh, well. It was time for new ones anyway."

"Ava! Save me from what?" Tension pounded against the inside of her skull like a child pounding on a locked door.

"Zachary. Yourself. This nasty family. Take your pick."

"I'm a big girl. I think I can handle the situation."

"A big girl? Is that why you're still dressed up as me?"

"You're going to ruin everything."

"What's to ruin? Let's switch back, go downstairs, and tell him."

Audrey's stomach contracted as if she'd just been punched. "I was just about to tell him when you showed up. I can't tell him now, not with you here. He'll flip out."

Ava waved her hand in the air, then leaned backward onto her elbows. "Aw, he'll get over it. He has a good sense of humor."

Audrey thought about last night in his cabin, about the hot, steamy moments under that quilt. She recalled his words on the way home. The truth promised to be hard enough without her sister here, muddying up the water. "I don't think so, Ava. I don't think he'll understand at all."

"Oh. My. God." Ava sat up straight. "You're in love with him, aren't you?"

Audrey blushed, and didn't bother denying it. Her sister knew her better than anyone.

Ava stood. She paced the room. "This isn't at all like you, Aud. *I'm* the one who gets into crazy situations." She paced some more. "You need to tell him the truth."

"You don't think I know that? Why are you

acting so virtuous? Normally, something like this would just be a game to you."

Ava turned to stare out the window. "You're not like me. You're the good girl, the honest one."

Guilt enveloped Audrey like a heavy blanket. Her relationship with Zach had been a lie from the very start. "I'm scared for him to know who I really am," she said quietly.

"That's stupid. You've always been too hard on yourself."

Audrey gestured toward her sister. "Look at you. You look fantastic. You even look better as *me* than I do." Ava sat again. Audrey sighed and joined her on the bed. "I love him, sis."

"Audrey, listen to me," Ava said gently. "I've known Zach for a few years now. He goes through girlfriends faster than I go through shoes." She laughed without humor. "A lot of those women probably were in love with him, too."

"But was he in love with them?"

Ava swiveled on the bed, wrinkling up the bedspread. "Did he tell you...?"

Audrey blushed and nodded.

Ava didn't say anything for a long time.

Finally, Audrey couldn't take it anymore. "What? He tells every woman he's in love with her, is that it? I'm nothing special?"

"No, Aud," Ava said, meeting her gaze. "I don't know that he's ever told anyone that."

Audrey's stomach did a happy cartwheel...then twisted into a knotted mess.

"Well. This complicates things a bit, doesn't it?" Ava lay back on the bed, staring up at the beamed ceiling.

Audrey joined her. "Yeah. A bit." How could she ever tell Zach that he'd fallen in love with a lie?

CHAPTER 11

The twins descended the grand staircase together about thirty minutes later.

"How can you walk in those things without falling?" Audrey motioned to Ava's black stiletto sandals, glad to be back in her own clothes again. Her comfortable flats sure made the steps easier to navigate.

Ava shrugged. "I don't even think about it."

Audrey stopped her sister with a hand on her arm when they were halfway down the stairs. "I can't do this."

"Aud, it'll be fine. You'll see. Just be honest with him. You're good at that."

"What if he doesn't understand? What if he—?"

Zach appeared in the foyer below.

"Give me a few minutes with him, okay?" Audrey whispered. "I'm going to throw up."

"Everything will work out fine."

Audrey wasn't so sure, and was even less sure when Zach's gaze went only briefly to her, then landed on Ava. And stayed there.

"Hello, ladies." His voice, the one she yearned for and cherished, coiled through her soul like a warm embrace.

Pain flooded her when he stepped beside Ava and slipped his arm around her waist, drawing her close. "I missed you," he whispered into Ava's ear.

Shards of jealousy stabbed her in the heart, even though she knew it was unfounded. In Zach's mind, he cozied up to the woman he thought he was in love with. Ava.

Audrey willed back threatening tears.

Ava gracefully extracted herself from Zach's embrace, and stepped toward Audrey. "Sis? You forgot to bring your bags downstairs. Zach, could you carry them down for her?"

"You're not staying, Audrey?" Zach looked directly into her eyes.

A part of her wanted to shout for joy at how he called her by her own name. She glanced at Ava. "Uh, no. I'd planned to, but something came up at home."

He smiled at her the way people smiled at distant acquaintances. "Well, you're more than welcome to stay." His gaze narrowed, and something flitted through his eyes. Suspicion? Recognition? "Uh, we have plenty of room."

She glanced away, fearing he'd see the truth before she was ready to provide it. "Um, thank you. My, ah, bags are upstairs. I'll show you."

She turned toward the staircase, but not before she saw Zach's arm snake around Ava's waist and pull her in for a quick kiss. Ava turned her head at the last minute, and he got her cheek. "My lipstick," she muttered.

Audrey couldn't see Zach's expression, but pictured annoyance flickering through his beautiful eyes. But he reached out and caressed Ava's waist before turning to Audrey.

He caught her watching and a sheepish, darling grin spread across his handsome face. "Sorry. I can't keep my hands off her."

Audrey pasted a fake smile on her mouth that trembled at the corners. She headed up the stairs in front of him, wanting to cry.

"Ava tells me you're a teacher," he said behind her as they reached the landing. The hallway to her room was wide enough that they could walk side by side, but she made sure to stay slightly ahead of him to avoid his gaze.

"Yes," she said.

"Junior high, right?" At her nod, he chuckled. "The hellish years. You must love kids."

She opened the door to her room, and stood aside for him to enter. "What's not to love?" She wanted to see his reaction to her words, to see if he felt the same way. But he'd walked over to the window and peered outside.

Her lungs expanded like an overblown balloon inside her chest until she couldn't breathe. Her gaze caressed him as he stood with his back to her, from his black, wavy hair that her fingers yearned to ruffle, to his broad shoulders that had loomed over her as they made love, to his arms that had wrapped around her and made her feel special and complete. She loved every single bit of him, from his head to his feet. She couldn't put this off any longer. She opened her mouth to blurt out her confession.

"How is it that you and your sister are so different?" he asked.

She stood frozen in the middle of the room, like he'd just pressed 'pause' on the Audrey remote. She gave herself a mental shake and held back a sigh. "If I had a dime for every time I've heard that question..." she said wistfully, crossing to the bathroom and stuffing Ava's makeup into the huge specialized carrier. She wouldn't need that any more. Ava could take it back to Boise with her.

"I'm sorry," he said. "I didn't mean anything by it."

She shrugged, even though he was in the other room and couldn't see. "Don't worry about it," she said. "Just give me a minute to get my things together."

She met her reflection in the bathroom mirror, the face that had greeted her daily up until a few days ago. Minimal makeup, hair pulled back into a slick ponytail. No jewelry. Simple clothes. She was who she was. Nothing more.

She closed the makeup case, bigger than her

overnight bag. Entering the bedroom, she found Zach hadn't moved from the window. How could he look so good wearing a simple, untucked white T-shirt and faded blue jeans? Her fingers curled and uncurled. She ached to touch him.

She had nothing else to pack, no excuse to keep him to herself any longer. She set the case beside the others near the door, then wiped her sweaty palms on her beige capris, ready to get it over with.

He turned toward her as she was about to speak. "It was nice of you to come all this way just to make sure Ava's okay. You two must be very close."

"We are." *Tell him!*

"Is it true what they say about twins?" he asked. "Do you and Ava share everything?"

A threesome flashed through her mind, and she inhaled sharply. "What?" she snapped.

Comprehension dawned on his face, and he laughed. "Oh, God. I'm sorry. Not that. Ava is quite enough for me."

Meaning, he couldn't imagine ever being turned on by *Audrey*. But she couldn't help smiling. Ava, meaning herself, was enough woman for him.

"I meant, I figure Ava's shared with you that she and I have known each other for a few years, and maybe she's told you of my...well—" His face reddened. "That she's shared with you my reputation." He cleared his throat. "I just wanted to assure you that I care a great deal about your sister. And that a person's reputation isn't always completely accurate, and I—" He cleared his throat again. "I adore your sister, and would never do anything to hurt her."

He looked away, and picked up the suitcase at the end of the bed.

"Do you love her?" Audrey asked, then held her breath.

He stared down at his feet. When he finally looked up, his eyes shone with emotion. "With all my heart, Audrey. Ava's everything I've ever wanted in a woman. I wouldn't change a single thing about her."

Audrey's heart swelled and ached at the same time. *He wouldn't change a thing about her?* A quiet sob hiccupped in her throat. Oh, God. How could she tell him the truth right now, when she was dressed as herself, someone he clearly wasn't attracted to?

A tear slid down her cheek, and she sniffled.

"Are you okay?" Zach asked, his expression both concerned and puzzled.

Please don't look at me like that.

She turned and brushed the moisture away. "Could you ask Ava to come up here, please?"

After a moment, he nodded, grabbed her bags, and left.

Audrey drew a shaky breath. One more switch of identities, then it would be over.

****

Zach placed Audrey's bags by the front door. His parents' driver would bring her car around, and load her bags when she was ready to go.

He stood in the middle of the foyer, staring up the staircase. Audrey had stayed behind in the bedroom, presumably to freshen up.

He glanced toward the great room, hearing Ava's voice.

Although the women shared similar physical attributes, they couldn't be more dissimilar. He looked forward to getting to know Ava's sister better. She'd driven three hours to make sure her sister was okay. Very kind-hearted. She'd cried when he mentioned his feelings for Ava. Clearly, she was a softie.

He headed into the big room, and saw Ava seated at one of the high-backed leather chairs, sipping an amber-colored drink. Her long legs were crossed at the ankles, and her short skirt rode up high on her thighs. His brother-in-law tried his best not to look at her legs and cleavage. Theresa and his mother had their pert little noses up in the air, full of disdain as they ignored her.

Zach sighed. Ava had done her job well. His family hated her. Unfortunately, as he hoped to make her his real fiancée, they had some mending of fences to do with his family. A lot of mending. Even though he didn't spend much time with them, it would make things easier if they learned to accept her.

Ava met his gaze, her face etched in worry. At least it looked like worry. Maybe she tired of being left to the Banister sharks all by herself. She rose and hurried across the floor, meeting him before he'd come halfway into the room.

He grinned as if to say her white knight had arrived. All the worry melted from her face, and she smiled back. He couldn't wait to get her alone. Finish what they'd started in his cabin. His grin broadened.

"Why are you so happy?" she asked. "Where's my sister?"

"I'm happy because you're here," he said, tugging her into his arms. "And Audrey is upstairs. She wants you to go up there. She got pretty emotional when I told her how I feel about you."

He ran his hands over her shoulders and down her back, but she stepped out of his embrace. She didn't quite look at him, and her expression seemed forced. Concern crept up his spine.

"Ava? Is everything okay?"

"Fine. Be right back." She fled the room before he could say another word.

He noticed his family watching with interest. Anxiety sluiced through his system as he wondered if perhaps Ava didn't share his depth of feelings. Just because she said she was in love with him, and acted like she was in love with him, didn't mean she really was. Appearances, after all, could be deceiving.

****

Audrey heard the door to her room open and close. Before she could worry that Zach had returned and caught her as she prepared to betray him for the last time, she heard Ava's voice.

"Aud, what happened? You didn't tell him yet, did y—" Her words cut off midsentence as she approached the bathroom doorway. "What are you doing?" she asked, her voice slow and amazed.

"What does it look like I'm doing?" Audrey shot back as she attached the fake eyelashes to her upper lid line.

"I can see *what* you're doing. The question is, why?"

"I couldn't tell him, Ava. He was going on and on about how perfect you are, how he wouldn't change a thing about you. How could I tell him that *I* was none of those things?"

"*You* are what he wants, Aud. You need to trust that."

Audrey shook her head, meeting her sister's gaze in the mirror. "I don't."

"So you're just going to keep pretending to be me? For how long?"

"Until after you leave. Until I figure out exactly what to say." Audrey turned, waving her hands in a shooing motion. "Hurry up. Change back."

"What?"

"Change back into me. I laid my clothes on the bed."

"Audrey. You're scaring me."

"He's going to suspect something if we don't get down there."

"This is ridiculous. *You're* ridiculous."

Audrey spun to face her, her hands clenched. "You got me into this mess. The least you can do is help me get out of it."

"But you *are* telling him today, right? I don't

want to go back to work Tuesday and have to pretend I'm in love with him, just because you're a coward."

Audrey sprayed hairspray onto her hair. "I promise I'll tell him. But it's going to hurt him, sis. And that just," Her voice caught, "kills me. I need to find the right time, the right place."

"There is no right time or right place. Just do it."

Audrey's stomach soured as she envisioned his possible reactions, none of them good. "I will." She used the hand-held mirror to make sure every angle looked perfect, that everything looked just like Ava. "Please do this for me? You owe me."

Ava looked for a moment like she would argue. Then she began stripping from her clothes. When she was done, she sat on the edge of the bed in her lacy bra and thong, watching Audrey's transformation.

A few minutes later, Audrey was ready to go downstairs and face Zach again. Anxious for him to wrap his arms, and love, around *her,* not Ava. God, she hoped he'd still *want* to wrap his arms around her.

She realized Ava hadn't finished dressing. "I'm going downstairs now, okay? I'll see you back in Boise?"

Ava sighed and crossed the room. "You look good as me, Aud. Really good."

Audrey relaxed. "Thanks, sis."

"But you're *not* me. You're you." Ava turned and headed toward the bathroom, pausing in the doorway. "I think you might have forgotten that." She shut the door behind her.

****

Zach wondered if he'd slipped into the seventh circle of hell as his brother-in-law droned on and on about the state of the bond market in today's economy. His sister and father listened intently, nodding at appropriate times and actually looking interested. Zach yawned, not bothering to cover it with his hand.

Two slender arms snaked around his waist, and warm breath fanned the back of his neck.

He turned around. "Hey, dollface. What took you so long?" He dipped his head and kissed her upturned mouth. Her arms wrapped around his neck, and she kissed him back with all the passion he felt roiling in his soul. Not even his dad's throat-clearing stopped him. He needed to get her alone.

Coming up for air, he noticed she'd come downstairs by herself. "Where's your sister?"

"She'll be down in a minute."

"Is she staying for dinner? It's almost ready."

Ava glanced away. "I'm not sure. I don't think so." She grabbed his hand, and led him out of the room.

"Where are we going?"

"Where can we go that's private?" she asked.

Desire wound its way up his spine as he followed her, guessing what she had in mind. "Over here."

He tugged her into the first-floor powder room, a room full of mirrors, marble, and clear light bulbs. He kicked the door shut with his heel.

"Zach, I need—"

He shoved her against the counter. "I need that, too, baby," he muttered against her lips as he thrust his tongue inside her mouth. "Now."

Lust coursed through his veins as he swallowed her moans, and her hands balled the shirt over his chest. She'd read his mind about wanting to be alone. Without breaking the kiss, he spun their bodies around and lifted her onto the counter. Her short skirt bunched up around her hips, and he hooked her legs around his waist.

He moved aside her collar and pressed hot, wet kisses onto her neck and cleavage.

Her fingers dug into his shoulders. "Zach, we

can't do this right now."

"Sure we can, dollface. We just need to hurry."

Her hands on his wrists stopped him as he reached for his fly. "No. Stop."

The tears in her eyes just about killed him. "Baby, what's wrong?"

"I'm so in love with you," she said, her voice catching. His heart burst at her confession. "But I'm scared, because I—" A tear slid down her cheek. "Because I—"

He pressed a finger to her soft lips, then replaced it with a kiss. "I'm scared, too," he said, tasting her salty tears. "And I'm so in love with you, too." He kissed her until little sounds of pleasure echoed in her throat. When she wrapped her arms around his neck, he unzipped his jeans and freed himself from their confines. Her thigh-high stockings presented no barrier to his need, and he quickly pushed himself into her ready heat. She gasped and arched her neck as he filled her up.

"Oh, baby," he groaned against her shoulder. "You're killing me."

She squeezed her thighs together, drawing him deeper inside. He thrust into her over and over, harder and harder until they climaxed together. He swallowed her moans of ecstasy with his mouth. His family might suspect why he and Ava had disappeared, but they didn't need their suspicions confirmed by her passionate cries.

After a few moments of afterglow, with his arms wrapped tightly around her and her hands pressed into the counter behind her hips, they pulled apart.

"My God, Ava. I don't think I could love you any more than I do right now."

She lowered her chin to her chest. "Is this just about sex, Zach?" she murmured, her gaze downcast.

With his finger, he tipped her face up to peer into her gorgeous eyes. "You don't honestly think that, do you?"

After a moment, she shook her head.

"Ava. Yes, I love the sex." He grinned. "But I love *you*. I love everything about you. Okay?"

Tears spilled onto her cheeks. She squeezed her eyes shut, but not before he saw her vulnerability and fear.

"Ava." He kissed her forehead.

A sob leapt from her throat.

"Oh, sweetheart." He kissed the tip of her nose. "I know we're moving fast. But don't worry. We'll figure it out."

Her shoulders shuddered. He wrapped her into his arms and held her tight. Her hands clutched his shoulders as if she feared she'd never see him again.

They reentered the main living area a few minutes later, hand in hand. Ava's flushed face told everyone present that they'd slipped away for some hanky-panky before dinner. Zach didn't care, and he couldn't stop smiling.

After some small talk with the family, and more than a few knowing looks from his father and brother-in-law, and even one from the dignified Stoudt, Zach tugged Ava into the corner of the room, to a shadowed area beside a large ficus. Her demeanor was as stiff as the old butler's posture. Obviously, his family still made her uncomfortable. He knew just what to do to prove to her his family's opinion didn't matter to him.

"I think we should make it official," he said, hearing the catch in his voice.

"Make what official?" she asked.

He lifted her left hand to his mouth, and kissed the backs of her fingers before holding the sparkling diamond up between them, the ring she'd been wearing just for show. Until now. "This."

Her free hand pressed over her chest, and her body trembled against his. "Wh-what?"

He kissed her hand again, then placed it over his heart. "I'm saying I love you, and want to be with you for the rest of my life." He held up his hand when she opened her mouth to speak. "Ideally, that means marriage and kids someday, but if you're not up for those things, I'm okay with that. I just want to be with you."

Her eyes widened and her mouth quivered at the corners.

"Holy Christ," muttered his father.

"Oh, my." That from Theresa.

"What the hell?" Allan sounded stunned.

Grace Banister merely gasped.

Zach turned, thinking they'd overheard his whispered proposal.

His family, every one of them, stared slack-jawed toward the doorway. Then they turned as a unit to stare at him and Ava.

"What's going on?" Ava murmured, and both she and Zach moved out of their corner to see what was causing all the fuss.

Zach blinked. Ava stood in the doorway. He turned to the woman beside him. And Ava stood right next to him, their fingers still entwined. He released her hand, and had the vague notion of it falling to her side. He barely registered her gasp.

"What is going on?" thundered Garrett.

"Audrey?" Zach asked, looking at the woman in the doorway.

"Don't look at me," she said, pointing to Ava beside him. "Talk to her."

Zach's brows pulled together, and a knot of something very uncomfortable began to coil in his gut. He turned to the woman beside him. "What's she talking about?"

Tears welled in Ava's eyes. "*She's* not Audrey," she said, pointing to her sister. "I am." She placed a hand on his arm. "Could we go someplace private to talk about this?"

Zach grabbed her shoulders and peered into her eyes. Guilt flickered in the green depths. *No!* His stomach muscles clenched as if he'd just been sucker-punched. "Who did I just spend the weekend with?"

The woman who was apparently Audrey blinked a couple of times. "You can't tell?"

He released her, feeling a wall close off around his heart. "Enlighten me."

Audrey glanced at her twin as if to draw her support, but Ava stood fast in the doorway. No help there. "It was me," she cried, tears falling down her face. "You spent the weekend with me. Please. Could we go somewhere—"

"No. I think right here is just fine."

"Will somebody please tell us what the hell is going on?" demanded Garrett.

Everyone ignored him, absorbed in the unfolding scene, which wrung out Zach's soul and left it dry and crumpled.

"Go on," he said to this Audrey, a woman he apparently didn't know at all. "I'm all ears."

She twisted her hands in front of her and once again looked to her sister. Out of the corner of his eye, Zach saw Ava nod. "When you asked Ava here for the weekend, she, um, was under the impression that—" She looked over his shoulder to his fascinated family. "Are you sure you want to do this here?"

He glared at her, refusing to let her quaking voice get to him.

"Okay. Um...anyway, remember how Ava was under the impression that you wanted her to be your *real* fiancée, and didn't hear the part about you just wanting a fake girlfriend for the weekend?"

Zach waited for his family to explode into applause, but to their credit, they remained silent.

"Ava's always had a hard time breaking it off with men, so she asked me to do it for her. I figured I'd break up with you that first night and go home, with you none the wiser, but then you—" Her voice caught, and she looked away. "But then you proposed, and no one's ever proposed to me before, and I couldn't say no, and...well, you know the rest."

"So this has all just been a game to you." He kept his voice flat, emotionless.

"No! I mean, at first it was, but everything we shared, everything we—" She glanced away, "—talked about, was real." She curled and uncurled her hands around each other, holding them over her heart.

He stared at her face, waiting for her to meet his gaze. When she did, he had to steel himself against the torment in her eyes. Her beautiful, deceitful eyes. "I don't believe you."

More tears cascaded onto her cheeks. He wouldn't let it bother him. She was no better than the women who'd come before her.

When he'd taken a few steps away, when he'd created enough distance between them that he wouldn't be tempted to touch her, he said, "I want you and your sister gone within the hour."

He shoved his hands into his pockets and strode out of the room, past the gaping mouths of his family, avoiding their looks.

Ava—the real Ava—still stood on the step. She wore the same stunned expression as everyone else. As he passed her, he said, "Ava?"

She looked up, expectant.

"You're fired."

CHAPTER 12

Audrey stood frozen except for the stream of tears sliding down her cheeks. No one in the room moved.

Finally, Ava came over and took Audrey's arm. "Come on. Let's get your things."

Audrey let herself be led across the room, past Zach's family who, amazingly, hadn't said a word. She paused at the threshold to the foyer. "I'm really sorry," she said, her voice tight. "I never meant for this to happen." She swiped at a tear with the back of her wrist. "I never meant to hurt Zach. I...just wanted you to know that."

She pulled the diamond ring from her left hand and approached Theresa. She held out the ring. "Could you please give this to your brother?"

Theresa took it, and their gazes connected for the briefest of moments. Theresa's mouth pressed into a small, sympathetic smile. Audrey followed her sister out of the room, moving like an automaton as they headed upstairs.

As soon as Ava shut the bedroom door, Audrey collapsed into a heap on the floor beside the bed, burying her face in her hands. She'd been so stupid. So stupid. And now she had nothing.

"That went well," Ava deadpanned.

Audrey sobbed through her fingers. "I blew it."

"Yeah, you did." Ava sat beside her, wrapping an arm around her.

Audrey suddenly remembered what had spurred the whole horrible scene, and pulled out of her sister's embrace. "*You* blew it for me. You ruined everything by coming downstairs dressed like that.

Everything would have worked out fine if you'd come down as me, like I'd asked."

Ava crossed her arms over her chest, silent.

"I would still be with Zachary, and he would still think I was—"

"He would still think you were what, Aud? This had to happen eventually. Maybe I shouldn't have forced your hand, but you kept talking yourself out of telling him. I was afraid you'd put it off until it was way too late."

"It's way too late now," Audrey whispered, amazed she could put a coherent sentence together when her entire soul felt ripped apart. "He looked at me like he hated me. Like he didn't know me."

Someone knocked on the door.

Audrey jumped up and sprinted across the room, stilettos and all. With hope lifting her heart, she flung open the door.

"I came to see if you needed anything, miss," Stoudt said.

Hope crashed and burned. She tried to smile, but her quivering mouth resisted. "Have you seen Zach?"

Stoudt glanced away briefly, and Audrey could tell the loyal and discreet employee battled with his humanity. Finally, he said, "I think he's showering."

Meaning he wanted to wash all traces of her from his body. She looked at the ceiling and resisted the tears.

She touched Stoudt's arm. "When you see him, would you tell him I'm sorry?"

Stoudt patted her hand, then backed up a step. "That is not my place, miss."

Her fingers curled around the edge of the door, and her ears hummed. "Oh. Of course."

"Miss Divine, er, Miss Thompson?" He reddened at the gaffe. "It was a pleasure serving you this weekend." His soft tone conveyed sincerity, and Audrey wanted to cry. He bowed. "Good luck, miss."

****

"I don't want to hear it," Zach snapped as he tossed his bags into the back of his Jeep. His heart felt like a sledgehammer had pounded it flat.

"Zach, if you could have seen her face—" Theresa began.

He gave her his most threatening look. "I. Don't. Care. And I can't, for the life of me, figure out why *you* do. You made your feelings about her very clear."

Theresa cleared her throat. "Yes, well, that was when she was pretending to be...someone else."

"You still don't know who she is. Neither do I."

"I know she cares about you, and the way you're acting tells me you care about her, too. *That's* why I care."

"You'll get over it."

She reached out and smoothed his hair from his forehead, like she used to do when she'd been his only mother-figure as a child. He jerked away, but she gave him that sympathetic look. "You love her, don't you?"

He ignored the knife through his heart. "Love is for movies."

"You realize this whole charade was your idea, don't you?"

"Whatever."

"She was only doing what you asked her to do."

Zach pointed his finger at Theresa's chest. "I asked *Ava* to help me out. I thought I was with *Ava*. Not Audrey. It was all a lie."

"Was it?"

He blew a sound of disgust between his clenched teeth. "Whose side are you on, anyway?"

She held up her hands. "Yours, of course. But Zach." She crossed her arms over her chest. "Think about something for a second, will you?"

He turned his head away, not caring.

"Why are you any better than Audrey in this

scenario? She's never played this game before, as far as I know. You and I have been doing it for years. I don't recall either of us stopping to consider the repercussions of our practical jokes on our parents. Do you?"

"Thanks for the morals pep talk, but I gotta go."

She grabbed his arm. He glared at her hand until she released him. "Maybe if you and I were strong enough to be honest with Mother and Dad over our relationship choices," She paused and rubbed her hands up and down her arms, "we could actually find someone we *truly* want to be with."

For the first time in years, his sister looked vulnerable, like the girl she used to be. Before Allan.

He shook his head. None of that mattered. Not any more. "I'm leaving."

"Where are you going?"

"Away from here."

****

The three-hour drive back to Boise dragged on and on. The scenery rushed past in a blur of blue and green and brown, partly because of Ava's fast driving, but mostly due to Audrey's tears.

She'd made a royal mess of things. If only she'd come clean when she'd learned Zach had asked Ava there as a phony fiancée. If only she'd never let herself be talked into this scheme in the first place. If only she hadn't let herself fall so madly in love. She sighed and stared out the window as rugged mountain peaks gave way to grassy plains.

If only.

If she'd never agreed to the scheme, she'd never have met him. And if she'd never met him, then she would never have known his love. But if she'd never fallen in love, she'd never have had her heart broken. She doubted it would ever completely mend.

Rain splatted on the windshield. Ava cursed as she turned on the wipers. "You said it never rains in Boise."

"We're not in Boise yet."

"It was sunny two minutes ago. Look, I can still see sunshine in the rearview mirror." Ava sounded almost as grouchy as she did.

"Tell it to Mother Nature," Audrey grumped. "Why are *you* in such a bad mood?"

"Oh, I don't know. Maybe because my sister lost the man she loves because of me, or because I lost my job. Take your pick."

Oh, God. She'd been so selfish, so wrapped up in her own misery, she'd ignored her sister's. "Oh, Ava," she said, turning in the seat. "It's not all your fault. I dug my own hole."

"Yeah, but you dug it with *my* shovel."

Audrey reached across the console and touched Ava's arm. "And I'm sorry about your job."

Ava shrugged. "I was getting kind of bored with it, anyway." She had never been one to wallow in self-pity for long. She pointed out the window. "Oh, look. A rainbow. See it?"

"Yeah, I see it." Audrey couldn't have cared less.

"Remember when we were kids, we'd ride our bikes really fast, trying to find the end of the rainbow?"

Audrey didn't say anything, even though she remembered those days fondly.

"Remember when we'd watch *The Wizard of Oz*?" Ava went on. "We'd fast-forward through all the boring black-and-white scenes, except for the rainbow song?"

"Yeah, I remember," Audrey said, her mind no longer on childhood memories. Her Technicolor moments had faded, and her boring black-and-white world—the one she'd tried to fast-forward through—had returned.

By the time they reached Boise, Audrey realized she didn't want to fast-forward any more. She liked her life—it just lacked a key ingredient. And she thought she knew a way to get it back.

Audrey pointed to a store. "Turn in there."

Ava grimaced. "Wal-Mart?"

"Don't be such a snob. I need to buy something."

Ava waited in the car while Audrey scurried inside. She found what she was looking for, then picked up a padded manila envelope, and rushed through the checkout line.

Back in the car, she pulled her purchase out of the bag. "*That's* what you were in such a hurry to buy?" Ava said. "I don't get it."

"It's for Zach. *He'll* get it," Audrey said, not bothering to tear off the label and price tag before sliding it into the envelope. "And if he doesn't get it, then he's not the man I think he is." She couldn't bear that thought.

She wrote his name in big block letters, then paused as she was about to write the address. "I don't know where to send it. What if he doesn't go home?" A smile curved her lips. "I'll send it to Stoudt. He'll know where to forward it."

"Today's Sunday, Aud. And tomorrow's a holiday."

Only a smidgen of air went out of Audrey's balloon. "Then I'll mail it first thing Tuesday."

****

As the four-wheeler bounced over the uneven terrain, Zach tried not to think about the last time he was at his cabin. With *her*.

Not thinking about her lasted about a millisecond.

He could almost feel her body pressed against his, her breasts crushing against his back every time they went over a bump.

Audrey. Audrey Thompson. He still wasn't used to thinking of her by that name. It fit her. It was nice. Normal. Just like—

He forced his concentration onto the beautiful scenery. She'd lied to him. He couldn't forget that. He *wouldn't* forget that.

Theresa's comments haunted him. Yes, *he'd* started the game, but Audrey had changed the rules. Once their relationship became real, she should have told him who she really was. But she'd continued to lie and betray him until he'd frigging proposed to her.

God! How could he have been so stupid?

Gray clouds spread across the sky, and tiny drops of water began to fall. Zach remembered how she had insisted on staying here last night because she'd been afraid to fly in the rain. That should have clued him in. He and Ava had flown in hellish turbulence before, and it hadn't fazed her.

He entered the clearing, and spotted the cabin nestled in the trees across the meadow. Normally, the first sight of his cabin brought a surge of warmth to his gut, a burst of happiness to his heart and soul. Now, however, he felt none of that. The cabin looked barren and desolate, its beauty faded.

First, she'd ripped his heart out and stomped all over it, which was bad enough. But now, *now* she'd ruined his favorite place in the world.

He cut the engine and yelled into the sky at the top of his lungs. The rain hit his face in increasingly sharper blasts until he was drenched to the bone, out of breath and completely hoarse.

His voice wasn't the only thing he'd lost, however. He'd also lost his dreams before they ever had a chance to begin.

CHAPTER 13

Zach lasted just four days at the cabin. By Thursday, his back and neck ached. He'd taken one look at the bed he and Audrey had shared, and knew he couldn't sleep there again. He'd slept in the chopper in the tiny, cramped space behind the seats where the luggage should have gone.

He arrived back in Sun Valley in a worse mood than when he'd left. The big house had an air of emptiness, his family long gone. Good. He didn't want to hear any more about Audrey, about the way she'd looked at him when she left, about how she'd cried. Blah, blah, blah. Bullshit.

As he entered the house, he wondered for the first time why he'd come back. Why hadn't he just flown to Manhattan?

Because Audrey's presence wasn't in New York, a little voice in his head told him.

God, he missed her.

His heart hardened in his chest, even while it twisted. No, he didn't. He couldn't miss someone he didn't even know.

He stopped in the doorway of the great room. Stoudt relaxed in one of the high-back chairs with the newspaper spread out before him, a glass of wine in one hand. On any other day, Zach would have enjoyed the sight, thinking of his parents' reaction were they to see it. But today, he just didn't give a damn.

Upon seeing him, Stoudt sprang to his feet. "Mr. Banister. I apologize for my liberties, sir. I was not expecting you."

Zach waved his hand and made a dismissing

sound through his teeth. "I'm not my parents."

Still, the butler looked frazzled, a reaction Zach had rarely seen in the man's long tenure with the family. "May I get you anything, sir?"

Zach started to shake his head, then said, "You could get me a beer. No, better idea. Why don't you join me? I'm going to get drunk."

"Sir?"

Zach cocked his head toward the kitchen. "Come on, old man. You know you want one."

Stoudt probably felt he had no choice but to follow. In the massive kitchen, Zach searched through the sub-zero fridge and found a six-pack. He tossed a can to Stoudt and popped the top on his own, then downed half of it in one long swig.

"Are you alright, sir?"

"I'd be better if you'd call me Zach." Wishful thinking. Such familiarity wasn't in Stoudt's breeding. He peered at the man over the top of his can. "Tell me something, Stoudt. What did you think of Ava—er, Audrey?"

"That's not my place to say, sir."

"I'm telling you it's your place." He downed the rest of the beer and reached for another one.

"Well, I'd have to say...I'd say she was delightful, sir."

Zach lowered the beer can. "Really?"

Stoudt's chest puffed out, and his chin lifted almost imperceptibly. "I think she's the only real thing in this unreal life of yours, and it would be idiotic for you to let her get away." He sipped his beer in the same way he did everything else—with dignity.

Zach almost laughed at the irony of the situation. Almost. "Okay, so *you* found her delightful."

Stoudt put down his beer. "Unless I am mistaken, it was only a few days ago that *you* thought she was delightful."

Zach wiped his mouth with the back of his wrist. "I think I liked it better when you weren't being honest, Stoudt."

The butler's brows rose, and he shot Zach a knowing glare that rivaled those of his parents. "As you wish, sir." He placed his can in a recycling bin in the pantry, then began wiping the granite counter tops even though they looked perfectly clean. Zach started to leave the kitchen.

"Oh, Mr. Banister. It nearly slipped my mind, but a package came for you." Stoudt picked up a manila envelope from the counter near the telephone. He handed it to Zach.

Zach stared at the envelope. He'd never seen Audrey's handwriting, but he knew it was from her even before noticing the Boise postmark. Part of him was tempted to toss it in the trash can on his way to the rest of his life.

But the other part of him, the part that ached, convinced him to see what she'd sent.

"I doubt it will bite," Stoudt remarked.

Zach shot him a withering look, then ripped the top edge off the envelope. He tipped its contents into his hand.

A DVD. His heart gave a lurch when he saw the title.

"*The Wizard of Oz*, sir?" Stoudt moved closer and hovered—something the butler had never been known to do. "That seems a rather...peculiar gift."

Snippets of his time with "Ava" flipped through Zach's memory. Her words—*What you see or think you see isn't always what you get, and what you get isn't always what you want*. The photo of herself— her *real* self.

Then he remembered his words to her—*She doesn't hold a candle to you, dollface*—and he wanted to groan. That must have broken her heart. All the times she'd referred to herself in third person. All the times she'd brought up her "sister."

She'd been trying to introduce him to the real Audrey.

He'd been such an idiot. She'd been sharing her true self with him all along. She'd even shared her greatest fear: being left behind when the balloon took off.

Hope surged through his soul, and his mouth tugged at the corners until he flat-out grinned. "No," he said to the faithful butler. "It's not peculiar at all, old man. It's...perfect."

****

Monday morning dawned clear and sunny. After several days of either gusty winds, rain, or both, today's calm was a refreshing change. Birds chirped outside Audrey's window. Still, the beautiful day didn't make it any easier to pull herself out of bed. But she had to. This was the last week of school. The thought of the entire summer looming ahead brought none of the usual anticipation.

Surely Zach had received his package by now. She had to start facing the facts: either he didn't understand the significance of her gift, or he didn't care.

He'd left her life for good.

Every morning, she woke up with hope that he'd call. Every night, she fell asleep with a pillow wet from her tears.

She needed to turn the channel on her misery. It simply would not do to finish the school year as a train wreck.

She dressed and prepared breakfast quietly, not wanting to disturb Ava, who slept on the pull-out couch in the living room. She smiled at the sight of her dead-to-the-world sister. Ava had been a godsend this past week, doting on her and listening to her go on and on about Zach and her shoulda-woulda-coulda's.

Starting today, she would quit feeling sorry for herself. She dumped her pity party down the disposal with the uneaten half of her waffle.

She drove to school with the windows down, the wind blowing through the car, and arrived at Treasure Valley Junior High an hour before the students were due. This would be a great week. She would just ignore that aching, empty place inside until she was at home tonight, alone in her bedroom.

She sorted through a massive stack of ungraded homework and end-of-year chores until her students burst in at the bell, their pre-summer excitement a boisterous counterpoint to her blue mood.

In the middle of first period, the school principal poked his head into the room. "Audrey, could you come out here a moment?" Rod cocked his head toward the hallway. "There's something you need to see. Kids, you might want to see this, too."

Puzzled, she followed him down the hall to the school's front entrance. Was it just her imagination, or did everyone stare at her? The kids trailed behind her as if she were the Pied Piper.

"Secret admirer, Audrey?" asked the school secretary.

A group of teachers had gathered in the front courtyard, looking toward the recreation fields.

Before she could see what had captured everyone's attention, Audrey felt something crunch beneath her feet.

Buttercups and violets littered the sidewalk.

Before she could process that, Rod nudged her in the arm and motioned straight ahead. A long, black limousine parked in the bus lane, and a man stood in front of it holding a sign.

"A friend of yours?" Rod asked, amusement in his voice.

Her heart skipped a beat. "That's Zach's butler. Well, his family's," she said, feeling dazed.

"Butler? Do people still have butlers?"

She walked close enough to read the sign. *Audrey Thompson*, it read, with an arrow pointing to the right.

With a tremulous smile at Stoudt, who didn't appear too butler-like with his ear-to-ear grin, Audrey turned in the direction of the arrow.

Her legs almost buckled. A rainbow-colored hot-air balloon sat smack in the middle of the soccer fields. Hope sped up her heart rate, and she glanced at Stoudt.

"You might want to run, miss. You don't want it to leave without you."

She stood on tiptoe and kissed his cheek, leaving a coral lipstick imprint on his pale cheek. She turned to Rod. "I'm sorry. I know it's the last week of—"

"We'll cover for you. You deserve this."

With one last look at everyone gathered on the school's front lawn, Audrey bolted toward the soccer field. Her hair flew free of its clip as she ran, and her shoulder-length locks whipped every which way.

She was about twenty yards from the balloon when Zach jumped out of the basket. They both stopped and stared at each other.

A smile radiated from Audrey's heart. Her chest heaved with excitement. *Zach.* Ripples of love shot upward from her toes like a firecracker. He looked wonderful. Tired and unshaven, but wonderful. Maybe he'd been as devoid of life without her as she'd been without him.

"I got your present," he said, his voice carrying over the dull roar of the balloon exhaust.

With perfect timing, they darted toward each other. Zach yanked her into her arms and kissed her cheeks, her eyelids, her forehead. "God. I've missed you."

Audrey closed her eyes and reveled in the feel of his warm mouth on her skin, his hard body enveloping hers. She skimmed her hands across his shoulders and down his back, pulling him tight against her heart. Right where she needed him to be. Forever. She pulled back and cupped his face between her hands. "It's really you," she said softly, tears threatening to flow.

"It's really me," he said.

"I'm so sorry," they said together, and laughed.

"This past week has been a nightmare for me," she said, reaching for his hands.

"For me, too."

"I want you to know I never, ever meant to hurt you." She entwined their fingers and squeezed. "Even though I was pretending to be someone else, everything we shared was real."

He raised their clasped hands to his mouth and kissed her knuckles. "I know. But it wasn't until you sent me the movie that I realized your appearance was the only thing about you that wasn't genuine. I love you, Audrey. Not your hair, your makeup, or your," His eyebrows rose, "your fake cleavage. Just you."

She blushed. "You don't mind the real me? Because what you see is pretty much what you get."

He tilted her chin up with his finger and peered down into her barely made-up face. "What I see is what I want."

"Yo! Rich guy!" called the balloon operator. "We gotta go."

Zach held up his hand to the impatient man, then slipped a ring onto Audrey's finger—a different ring than the one he'd given her a week ago, a beautiful solitaire on a simple platinum band. "This one suits the real you better. Beautiful. Not overdone," he said, then kissed her hand. "Come with me."

Hand in hand, they jogged to the balloon, then climbed into the basket. "Where are we going, Zach?" Amazingly, the thought of flying with him now induced no fear.

"Wherever the rainbow leads us."

She wrapped her arms around his neck, and lifted her mouth to meet his. A cheer rose from the ground as the balloon lifted off.

"Should I click my heels together three times?" she asked against his lips.

"No need, dollface," he said, tightening his embrace. "You're already home."

About the Author

Somewhere between raising two busy kids, battling an army of dust bunnies, and convincing her husband of 21 years that frozen pizza is really a health food, Rebecca J. Clark decided to put the characters in her head down on paper. Just to shut them up. Rebecca now lives in the Pacific Northwest where she loves creating fun and sexy stories for her readers. When she's not writing or doing mom stuff, she works as a personal fitness trainer and teaches group exercise classes. All this activity allows her to frequently indulge in her favorite hobby: chocolate.

Visit Rebecca at: *http://www.rebeccajclark.com*

Thank you for purchasing this Wild Rose Press publication. For other wonderful stories of romance, please visit our on-line bookstore at www.thewildrosepress.com.

For questions or more information contact us at info@thewildrosepress.com.

The Wild Rose Press
www.TheWildRosePress.com